MAP *of the* IMPOSSIBLE

A MAPWALKER NOVEL

J.F. PENN

Map of the Impossible. A Mapwalker Novel Book 3
Copyright © J.F.Penn (2020). All rights reserved.

www.JFPenn.com

ISBN: 978-1-913321-31-4

Requests to publish work from this book should be sent to:
joanna@CurlUpPress.com

Cover and Interior Design: JD Smith Design
Printed by Amazon KDP

www.CurlUpPress.com

"Pulvis et umbra sumus.
We are but dust and shadow."

Horace, The Odes

"There is nothing impossible to him who will try."

Alexander the Great

PROLOGUE

Fongafale, Tuvalu, South Pacific

The earth shook once more, a tremor more powerful than the last. A deep rumble sounded from beneath the ground as if the gods wakened in anger, and Meihani clutched a nearby palm tree with gnarled fingers to hold herself steady. The rough bark scraped against her skin as she tried to stay upright. She was old but a lifetime of walking the island had strengthened her limbs and as she braced herself, the shudder passed beneath her.

It would not be the last.

Something had changed in recent weeks, a shift in the cycles she had seen in her long life. The earth was broken — and they would all pay the price.

Meihani looked out over the waves to the horizon across the tiny cove. She stood just around the bay from where fishermen launched their boats, hoping that today would bring enough food for their families and maybe even some to sell at the market. She walked here each morning as first light struck the water and every day, she thanked the gods she was still alive. At her age, there was no guarantee she would greet the dawn once more.

Meihani breathed in the salty air, relishing every inhale

and exhale. She had witnessed the final moments of so many as an elder of the village. The wracking coughs of the old, the tiny sighs of the too-early born and too soon to pass. So many souls ahead of her on the ancient path and still each day she rose once more to greet the dawn. She said a prayer to the god of the ocean, her lips moving as she whispered words of thanks and supplication.

The waves were grey green, reflecting the thick clouds gathering above, and the sun hid behind a storm front, its light and power dimmed by a force that would sweep over the island before midday. Meihani could read the signs as easily as others read the newspapers that came over from the mainland. She understood the moods of the ocean and from this vantage point each morning, she could judge her daily walk.

On soft days, when the waves were gentle, she shuffled off her shoes and paddled in the water, sinking into the sand and wiggling her toes like she had done since she was a girl, delighting in the pleasure of sensation. On wild days, she would stand here by the thick palm, both of them grown strong over the years they dwelled on the coast. The wind could howl and the waves pound down, but she was safe up here as rain pelted the green leaves above her. On those days, she would remember how wild she had once been, surfing on a hand-carved board, diving amongst the rocks, almost made of seawater. The ocean was in her veins and Meihani knew it more intimately than any lover.

Today, something was very wrong.

The ground shook again with a deep rumbling under the earth. A horde of tiny crabs emerged from the sand, shaken loose from the golden grains. They scuttled for shelter under the palms up the beach, their skittering legs leaving tiny marks in the sand that were quickly shuffled away by movement from the depths beneath.

Meihani frowned. That was odd. The creatures should

have run for the waterline and sunk beneath the wet sand once more. Out in the open, they would be easy prey for the gulls, flipped over, legs wriggling while sharp beaks tore the soft flesh from their undersides as they were eaten alive.

She looked up, expecting to see eager birds wheeling toward the ready feast. But the flocks overhead flew inland to the hills, calling to one another with shrill notes on the edge of a scream. When birds and beasts fled inland away from the water, the danger was out to sea. This ancient wisdom had never failed her ancestors and Meihani knew she should hurry back to the village, tell them all to run for higher ground. She looked again to the horizon. Perhaps it was only a storm and besides, warnings from the old were rarely heeded unless danger was imminent. She would wait a little longer.

The tremors had been coming for days, some sharp blows that knocked her off her feet like the fist of her husband on nights when he had drunk his weight in beer. Others had been soft and gentle, like the arms of her loving mama. Both dead many years now, but neither forgotten. Meihani could still remember everything from back then, even though these days she often forgot where she put her glasses, or the names of her various grandchildren when they came so infrequently to visit from Fiji, a world away from her quiet life. Her body may be stooped and wrinkled, folded by time, but this physical frame would not cage her mind — and on this beach every day, she was briefly free. A spirit of the ocean once more.

Another rumbling deep below the earth.

A jolt. A dip as the ground seemed to fall away.

Meihani's stomach dropped, and she gasped as a terrible realization rose within. She looked back at the path to the village, knowing that her legs could not carry her fast enough now. It was too late.

The water receded with a wet sucking sound, leaving sea

creatures in its wake, like the ebb of the tide but so much faster. Parrotfish flopped on the sand and arched their spines in desperation for water, mouths gaping open. Jellyfish pulsed their last as they lay stranded next to coral-tinted cowrie shells. A turtle clawed at the sand, head poked out, eyes wide as it stared around in confusion.

The sea withdrew further, revealing sand and rocks that had never been uncovered before in Meihani's lifetime. Then the skeletal hull of a wooden boat, barnacles clustered on its spars, rainbow anemones dying as they met the air, colors fading quickly.

Still the water sucked back, further and further.

Words came on the wind, whispering to Meihani in her Mama's voice, spoken from her deathbed as she took her last breath. "If there is danger, child, cross over. The Borderlands will always welcome you."

Some thought the Borderlands were a myth, but Meihani knew there was a place off the edge of the map where displaced people could find a home. When she looked to the sea some days, she glimpsed what might be a shimmer of a veil between the worlds.

Many in her village could sense some kind of border out there, perhaps descendants of those who had crossed long ago, leaving some latent gift in generations to come. But in recent weeks, they had spoken in whispers of it closing, a sense that the barrier in the sky and in the ocean had become blocked. Some dismissed their words, others stored up provisions in case of disaster. But none had seen this coming.

Meihani gazed at the track toward the village. Her footprints still lingered in the dust, marks made every day for the span of a life. Times had changed, but the ocean remained her constant — and now she knew it would be her end. She turned away from the village, putting the past behind her, and looked out to the waves as they pulled back still further.

Their island was low-lying, one of many threatened by the rise of oceans and vulnerable to natural disaster. They had been encouraged to leave, but this was their home. There was nowhere else to go. Meihani had hoped to die before the end of the island, but it seemed like fate would entwine them in a lover's embrace.

She pushed away from the palm and walked slowly down the beach, kicking off her shoes and wriggling her toes in the wet sand. A smile transformed her features into those of a young girl once more. She relished each footstep, an imprint on the ocean floor that disappeared even as she walked on. Manoko fish died around her, flopping their last, as she picked a path through the arms of death.

She reached the ruins of the fishing boat and touched its spars. Her father had once sailed something like it, his face ever set to the sea. Sometimes he would let her go out with him and she would sit curled up in the bow and watch for dolphins, shouting with joy when they swam ahead, leaping before the wave. He always told her that the sea was their life and their death, and that was as it should be for an island people.

Meihani looked past the boat to where the water towered high against the horizon, sucked back into a giant wave the size of the American skyscrapers she saw on TV shows. Such a thing was incredible to behold, but those who saw it this close would never tell their tale. That was certain.

Part of her wanted to keep walking toward that wall of water, to welcome it with open arms like the wild teenager she had once been, screaming her fury into the storm. But the little girl inside was afraid.

Meihani reached up into the boat and pulled herself toward the bow. Her arms were weak but her old body was frail and light so it wasn't too difficult. The wood was wet and cold but she had spent much of her life that way, so it wasn't a hardship to curl up in the corner of the bow, her face toward the island that held so many memories.

The smell of salt and kelp filled the air as the roar of the ocean grew to a deafening sound. A rush of oncoming horses charging into battle, a hail of rain and thunder. The first drops of the tsunami fell upon her face. As it towered above, Meihani closed her eyes, her palms against the wooden hull beneath her as she waited for its final embrace.

* * *

BBC News Report

A tsunami struck the low-lying island of Fongafale in Tuvalu today in the aftermath of a deep-sea earthquake off the coast. The entire island remains underwater with several villages and a resort submerged by the flood. Casualties are reported to be in the thousands and no survivors have been found.

Military vessels from Australia and New Zealand converged on the area to help the Tuvaluan police recover bodies from the waves, but the operation has been hampered by ongoing tremors in the region and stormy weather conditions.

Geologists cannot explain why there has been such an increase in earthquakes and natural disasters in the last month.

"After the San Francisco Bay Area evacuation and now this South Pacific disaster, plans are underway to move people out of possible danger zones," Dr Willow Mackenzie said, speaking from James Cook University in Australia. "It's a daunting task on a global scale. Tectonic plates all over the globe seem to be rubbing up against a new barrier, shifting in ways we've never seen before. It's unprecedented, but we have a multi-disciplinary team working on mapping scenarios. We can say that this will not be the last natural disaster."

CHAPTER 1

SIENNA FARREN CLOSED HEAVY curtains over the tall Georgian windows, blocking out the light. It was raining and the buildings opposite were empty, but she didn't want any witnesses to what she was about to do.

The open-plan apartment above the map shop in Bath had been her grandfather's, handed down to her on his death, a casualty of the ongoing war between those who protected Earthside and the Shadow Cartographers of the Borderlands. Sienna hadn't been in the place long enough to make it her own, or perhaps she wanted to keep it intact in memory of the man she hadn't known well in life. She felt his presence in the bookshelves filled with his journals and art on the walls that reflected his passion for cartography. And of course, downstairs, in the collection of antique maps and globes, each a portal to those who could travel through. But the toll of magic tainted their promise, the stain of shadow in exchange for the gift of mapwalking — and that price concerned her now.

Sienna walked over to the full-length mirror in the corner of the room and pulled up her long-sleeved t-shirt to reveal her slim torso. She had inherited her grandfather's pale skin and titian hair and usually her stomach was lightly freckled, but now those subtle hues were lost in tendrils of black that formed patterns under her skin like tattoos of some ancient tribe.

The marks didn't follow the lines of her veins, but curled into beautiful shapes, almost like ink swirling in water, shifting with the movement of her body and even her mood. Some days they were faint, like the last days of a bruise. She could even make them disappear if she concentrated hard enough. But after a night of restless dreams, the marks had etched themselves deeper into her skin and begun their journey along her arms toward her neckline. These t-shirts would not hide the stain for long and Sienna feared what would happen when Bridget or her father or one of the other Mapwalkers noticed. She didn't want to face the possibility of what it might mean.

But the dreams were becoming more vivid.

Last night, she had dreamed of soaring amongst the clouds above the Borderlands, darting like a bird into the blue. She heard her name called from the Tower of the Winds in a voice of a thousand thousand souls.

Sienna.

The pull was almost irresistible, a longing inside her that echoed some elemental need. But as she drew closer, the tattooed lines of the city of Bath on her arms burned, a reminder of her promise to safeguard Earthside. She shifted in the air, tried to dive down toward the land below, tried to escape from the voice, but mist gathered about her and skeletal shapes of winged creatures with razor talons swooped close to ward her away from safety, herding her back to the Tower of the Winds. Closer, closer, until she could almost see what lay inside. She had woken with a gasp, heart pounding, sheets damp with sweat, and the marks on her skin had spread.

Sienna traced one of the dark whorls with a fingertip, touching her own skin as if it was a stranger's body. The marks were beautiful and yet, if anyone knew how deeply she was entwined with the Shadow, she would be sent to the medical wing of the Ministry. There were rumors of it, whispers of a ward filled with Mapwalkers in shadow coma, their bodies etched in black ink. Some recovered, others were lost.

It was the price of Mapwalker magic, a drop of shadow for every use. Those with too much could turn and become a Shadow Cartographer, powerful on the other side of the border but a sworn enemy to those on Earthside.

Or they must remain here, banished from ever crossing again, denied the place that brought them alive, denied the use of their magic for fear of what they might become. Like her father, a broken man, bled of his magic, afraid of the Shadow turning him, scared of it taking what was left of his life, and yet, still, he craved its touch.

But perhaps she was different, perhaps she could remain on the knife edge — but only if she kept the marks hidden. At least long enough to get back over to the Borderlands.

Sienna thought of Finn's dark eyes, the soft touch of his lips as he woke her from the shadow weave when she had last seen him. What was he doing now? She didn't know if he was alive, safe but on the run with the Resistance, or dead at the hands of his father, the Warlord, Kosai. She had to go back to find out whether they might have a future together — and to face the voice that kept calling in her dreams.

She pulled down her t-shirt and turned away from the mirror, reaching up to the bookcase for one of her grandfather's journals. He had traveled widely in the Borderlands, with years of experience as a roaming Mapwalker. His skin had been tattooed with the lines of Bath, as her own was now, but perhaps he had never heard the call from the Tower of the Winds. Or things had changed somehow. The balance undone by the shifting wheel of time and circumstance.

Every day, she scoured the pages of his journals for some clue as to how they could undo what had been done. She kept coming back to journal 24. It mentioned the Map of the Impossible, a way through the space between the worlds. Her grandfather had learned of it during one of his sojourns in the Library of Alexandria, perhaps from the lips of his lost love, the Librarian, but there were no specifics as to what it was or where it might be.

Sienna turned another page of the journal, sensing the throb of shadow beneath her skin. Perhaps today she would find the way back.

* * *

Mila Wendell put another log into her tiny wood-burning stove, pushed it deeper into the flames with a poker, and then shut the grate once more. Rain hammered on the roof of the canal boat, making it a snug haven down here below. The smell of cedar wood hung in the air, mingled with the scent of freshly roasted coffee. Everything was as it should be — but Mila couldn't deny the sense of unease that curled in her stomach.

When Bridget closed the border, there had been a moment of rest, a beat of silence, almost a numb realization amongst the Mapwalkers. They had stopped the invasion, saved Earthside from a devastating plague — but the sense of loss took her breath away, as if they had chopped off a limb. Mila wanted to fling open the gates again and consequences be damned. She had an inkling she wasn't the only one who felt that way.

Zippy, her golden cocker spaniel, whined a little and nuzzled up to her leg before settling on the rug in front of the stove. He put his head on his paws and looked up at her with patient eyes. Mila knew he would love to be out there running along the towpath, splashing in the puddles. They would go out later, whatever the weather.

She reached down to stroke his soft ears, scratching the places he loved. "Good boy. You sleep there for a bit."

She stretched as much as she could in the tiny space, raising her arms up so they pressed against the ceiling. The sound of rain on the roof and the smell of wood smoke and Zippy's rhythmic breath could usually anchor her, but Mila couldn't escape her sense of restlessness.

Was this truly her home, or would she feel more at ease somewhere else … with someone else? She thought of Ekon, his lithe, muscular body slipping ahead of her through the waters beneath Ganvié Island. The touch of his liquid skin under the waves as they swam together to the sunken tomb with the buried map.

Mila smiled at the memory, a bubble of joy welling up at the knowledge that there was someone else like her out there. Perhaps there were more in other corners of the Borderlands. In discovering the Mapwalkers, she had found a family and a purpose to her life, but in finding another Waterwalker, Mila had glimpsed a possible future. She couldn't go to Ekon now, but there was something she could do to feel closer to him.

She bent to the woven rug in the middle of the canal boat and pulled it back, revealing a trapdoor surrounded by a waterproof seal. She tugged it open with a squelch of rubber and looked down into the dark water of the canal lapping beneath. Zippy put his head up at the sound, ears perked, eyes questioning.

Mila reached over to stroke him again. "It's okay, boy. I won't be long."

She slipped off her clothes and sat on the edge of the hatch, dangling her legs for a moment. The water was cool against her skin in the moment of change, but as her limbs shimmered, she became part of the liquid and pushed off to sink below the surface.

As a Waterwalker, she could travel in the spaces between ripples along the watercourses of this world and beyond, her magic turning her into almost another being. But every time she used it, Mila felt that drop of shadow remain. Even now, lying here under the canal boat, she could feel it seep further into her. Each time she turned, it was harder to emerge into the world of air above.

As she sank into the canal, Mila felt a sense of relief, a welcome coolness as her body changed. She was increasingly out of place in the world above and she wondered if perhaps her people had never disappeared, but merely stayed in the water, invisible to those above. Did they become pure liquid after a time?

She had no real knowledge of the bloodline from which she came, raised by a foster mum in the high-rise blocks of East London. There were hints that her father had been a student from war-torn Sierra Leone, her mother too young to keep her. In London, her mixed-race heritage was normal, but here in Bath, her dark skin and almond-shaped eyes stood out. Yet under the water, she shimmered and became all the colors of the rainbow and yet, no color at all.

Mila slipped out from beneath the shelter of the boat into the channel of the canal. She darted up toward the lock, her body reveling in the freedom to move, however brief her time could be here. She gazed up through the green light to the world above, watching as the rain dimpled the surface. It was a moment of beauty but the canal was a tame playground, protected and safe with only a short distance to roam. The only danger was the discovery of her true nature which she kept hidden by her daily routine as a resident of the canal.

But this dual existence was becoming harder to maintain. Should she embrace life on the edge of this elegant city of Bath and truly make her home here? Or was she really a Waterwalker, meant to live under the waves in a land on the other side of the map? She could not do both, for that way, madness would lie in the constant longing for a different life.

A choice loomed ahead, and it would come for Sienna, too. Something had shifted for both of them on the last mission, and Mila sensed her friend was even more torn than she was. They both had one foot on either side of the border and it was slowly tearing them apart.

CHAPTER 2

Perry Mercator pulled himself up once more, muscles bulging as he touched the lintel of the door with his chin.

"14 … 15 …"

Sweat ran down his back, his breath ragged as he counted the repetitions, embracing physical pain as the best way to dull the screaming in his mind.

"29 … 30."

He dropped to the floor and bent over with exhaustion as he fought to regain his breath. Nausea rose in his stomach as his body rebelled at the harsh treatment, hours every day, pushing himself to physical extremes.

For most of his life, Perry's fire magic had been out of control — sometimes a tiny flame, sometimes an inferno — and yet on the last mission, he had finally found a way to channel it. He had saved the Mapwalker team at the Eagle's Nest, and in those moments, he had felt most alive. But the stench of burned maps still hung in the air of the corridors of the Ministry, a reminder of how fire had destroyed the very heart of the Mapwalker domain. Fire started by his father, Sir Douglas Mercator, a Shadow Cartographer, a traitor — a murderer.

After the death of the Illuminated Cartographer, Perry

had helped John Farren take the body out to an ancient Somerset hill overlooking Glastonbury. Under the light of the full moon, they built a pyre of old English oak and piled up the tattered remains of the ruined vellum and paper maps and burned books, the scraps of what had once been his home.

Perry lifted the body of the old man onto the logs and placed him in the middle of a nest of map fragments, his frame so wasted and thin that there was hardly anything left before the flames devoured what little remained. The Illuminated had always seemed so vibrant, so strong, but clearly, the maps had sustained him. His blood ran with ink and when he relinquished their hold, there was nothing left but a husk of flesh. He had lived many generations For Galileo, his name lost to time, but whoever he had once been, his legacy was certain in the strength of the remaining Mapwalkers.

Perry had started the fire with his magic, kindling the remaining pieces of the maps around the corpse. As the flames rose, he contained its heat and strength, making sure everything was destroyed. The stars shone brightly overhead, the air crisp and chill, and the smoke formed symbols and pathways as it rose, as if the old man traveled through a new map toward the heavens.

Now, weeks later, Perry ached to get back to the fight. The Mapwalkers had stopped the invasion and won the battle, but they had lost so much. Earthside itself was wounded and Perry knew the time ticked away until he would cross the border again. There was no way to regain what they had lost, only a path forward to a different future.

He jumped and hung on the doorframe once more before pulling himself up to start the next set.

"1 ... 2 ... 3 ..."

When he faced his father again, he would be ready.

* * *

Bridget Ronan sat at her desk in the library surrounded by a billowing sea of maps. As she reached for the next volume of the Mapwalker annals, the vellum and paper moved with her. She could feel their weight on her body — pressing down against the mercurial flights of her mind.

An anchor some days. A prison on others.

Some days her new role as the Illuminated Cartographer didn't seem real, and she tried to walk out the door of the library, striding toward freedom, only to be jolted back, held tightly by the maps that wound themselves into her flesh. The ink that now ran in her veins meant she could never leave this place again. She had traveled the world and the lands beyond and yet, she could now only sense it through the maps here in this room. Her world was at once constrained and yet also of unlimited possibility.

After the night of the fire, Bridget wondered if the Ministry was wounded beyond repair. But not all the maps had been destroyed in the flames that Sir Douglas had set, and the memory of many more ran through the ink that now mingled in her veins. In the weeks since, she had questioned her choice many times. But had there really been a choice? The maps could not live without an Illuminated, a Blood Mapwalker, and the death of the old could only mean a new one must be bound to the cause.

John had told her of the pyre he and Perry built under the stars for the old man. How the smoke had carried his spirit away. Bridget wondered if one day someone would do the same for her, whether she would last as long, and whether her name would also be lost over the generations ahead.

It wasn't clear how long the old man had been the Illuminated, but the line was unbroken, the position assumed and lived with no record of who each had been before. Eventually her own name would be erased. She would only be the Illuminated, tied to the maps for generations to come. Perhaps she would even forget what she had once been.

Memories came to her through the ink, memories held by the Illuminated Cartographers before her, remnants of what they had seen. Bridget understood that each time she accessed them, part of her own life crumbled away, dissolving into the ink.

Some days she raged against her captivity, wishing she had a flame so she could finish what Sir Douglas had started. Other days, she closed her eyes and roamed into the maps, traveling in her mind further than she had ever been able to do in person.

Over the last weeks, Bridget had called for a renewal of the map library. She sent requests to the other Ministries around the world, asking for copies of everything they had. She had used funds to buy originals from antique map houses in Istanbul and Amsterdam, needing to build the library back up but also to expand her world once more.

Truthfully, she did not know what she was doing, but she trusted that the maps of the world held everything she needed. There was wisdom in the maps and a vestige of magic in the ink that flowed through her. She just didn't know how to wield it yet.

Had the old man learned his role from a previous incarnation of the Illuminated? Or did he have to learn as she did from the very beginning? Perhaps her predecessor had not chosen this path either. Perhaps it was only ever unwillingly pressed upon the next.

Bridget sighed and opened the volume of annals, turning the pages and scanning the text as she continued her search for a way to open the border once more.

Suddenly, she stopped, her attention caught by a drawing sketched on the ivory paper. Its bold lines portrayed a figure whirling within a vortex of shadow and light, the face obscured by a silver mist surrounded by drops of scarlet.

A faint scent wafted up, a memory of flame. Bridget bent closer to the page to examine the medium and then drew back with a frown.

Ash and blood. Smoke and magic. But what did it mean?

"Look what I found." John's voice interrupted her from the outer room of the library and Bridget turned in greeting.

He pulled out a rolled map as he walked around the corner, still limping and bowed, his injuries a permanent reminder of how the Mapwalkers had failed once before.

"It's Buondelmonti's Constantinople from 1422. The only surviving map predating the Turkish conquest." John placed the scroll down on the desk and gently unrolled it. "The Bibliothèque Nationale in Paris sent it over. On loan, of course, but I thought it might brighten your day."

He smiled at her and in his blue eyes, Bridget saw a glimmer of the man he had once been, his head thrown back in laughter as they danced on the edge of a silver lake in the Uncharted, together for a brief magical moment. She smiled at the memory, bittersweet with the knowledge that they would never again walk those trails together. She was trapped here and the man he once was had been bled out of him, cut away by a Shadow Cartographer in the dungeon of a dark castle.

John had lost more than his blood down there and he could never cross the border again. Even if he could, Bridget didn't think he would go. He once had the confidence of the true Blood Mapwalker, one who could wield his power against the Shadow and win — but no longer. She only hoped his daughter could find her way to true power.

Bridget bent down to examine the map more closely, the waters of the Bosphorus in a faded green with ramparts of the walled city of Constantinople ringing its shores in shades of umber.

"It's beautiful, thank you." She gestured toward the racks of newly built shelving. "Put it on the third shelf down.

That's my to read pile — once we get through the rest of the annals." She pointed to the stack of thick books by her desk. "We've still got hundreds of years to trawl through."

John carefully rolled the map up with gentle fingers and laid it on the rack. He sat down next to the desk and pulled the next volume off the pile of annals.

"We'll find something. The answer has to be in these somewhere." He dusted the cover off, opened the front page and began to read.

Bridget watched him in companionable silence. John came every day to sit in the library and read by her side as they scoured the archives for anything that might help with the border. When it closed, they had not realized the ramifications. But the world beyond deteriorated, earthquakes, tsunamis and people dying because they couldn't cross over. The Borderlands were home to many; they were an escape to many more. Now they knew that Earthside needed an escape valve, a way to release the pressure — and neither world could exist in isolation.

Bridget stared down at the figure sketch in ash and blood. John had barely glanced at it in the excitement of the rare Constantinople find, so perhaps it was nothing. But blood had always been at the heart of Mapwalker history.

There were family trees in the scrolls, but over time, many of the bloodlines had dwindled in power. Those on Earthside truly had nothing to compete with what the Shadow Cartographers did on the other side of the border: forcible breeding across magical lines to create original forms of magic. There were also tales of a drug given to pregnant women to encourage mutation in children born away from the Fertility Halls, in the hope that nature would produce new kinds of power.

As abhorrent as the practices were, Bridget understood why they did it. Every day more children of magic were born over there, some powerful, some destined to work the mines or fight as soldiers, some discarded as worthless. It was relentless and if things didn't change, those on Earthside would be outnumbered within a generation.

But the border was the most immediate problem. They closed it to stop the plague coming over in a wave of refugees, but now that seemed like a terrible mistake. In closing the border, they doomed Earthside to an acceleration of natural disasters. They had to find a way to open it again.

Bridget pulled the next volume from the stack and began to read once more.

CHAPTER 3

FINN PAGE PULLED HIS cloak tighter against his body, wrapping the black material around his sword to hide any glint of metal. He stood motionless in the shelter of a temple wall as a band of soldiers ran past through the narrow streets, the half-moon of the Shadow Cartographers tattooed on their faces, the banner of the wolf's head held high above them. As they rounded the corner of the street and their footsteps faded into the noise of the trader town, Finn shook his head and sighed. That had been much too close.

The price on his head was so high now that he had started to doubt even close members of the Resistance. His father, the Warlord, Kosai, offered riches and status to anyone who would turn him in, alive or dead, so he had to remain vigilant, only walking the streets when he really needed to.

Finn pulled out the vial of blue liquid from within his shirt pocket and swirled it around, inky darkness mixing with a lighter teal within. He hoped this had been worth the risk.

He set off through the warren of dirt streets, staying away from the thoroughfare of the trader town. The city was said to have no name because no one stayed long enough to call it home. Refugees arrived on its stinking shore, drifting across the ocean from Earthside to be swept up by the slave traders and sold to the mines or sent to the Fertility Halls — at least, they had arrived that way until the border closed a month ago. The trader town had emptied after days of watching the becalmed sea and now only a few slavers waited by the beach just in case, while the rest had gone to raid villages on the outer edges of the Uncharted. The tide of new arrivals had stopped altogether on that fateful day.

The last time he had seen Sienna.

Finn remembered her face that night, bruised and muddied but still beautiful, her titian hair streaming down behind her as she told him of her plan. The only way to stop the plague crossing over to Earthside was to close the border.

He had not believed it possible, but she had surprised him once again. Just as she had in the dungeons of the Fertility Halls where she had helped him find his sister moments before her bloody end. It was possible that Sienna's magic was much stronger than even she knew, and as much as he wanted more, Finn felt the distance between them might now be too wide a gulf.

He had fled the camp that night, guilt chasing him even as he ran through the sea of rats, leaving behind thousands of refugees to die of the plague. There was nothing he could do for them and it was better to live another day than die from the bites of plague-ridden rodents or under the swords of his father's men.

Flashes of memory from that night still haunted his dreams. Hordes of rats gnawing on the half-dead. A silver-haired girl with arms raised high, clawing life energy from those around her while mutants from the Shadow roamed the corpse-strewn camp, finishing any left alive. There was powerful magic on both sides of the border, but he was one of the majority who were merely human. Finn could only think that his role was to stand against the darkness as much as he could. The Borderlands were his world and he could not wait for the Mapwalkers or anyone else to save his people.

The Resistance had grown in the wake of the plague and mass murder of those in the camps. News had spread of the culling of infected refugees, the indiscriminate destruction of those considered useless once the invasion proved impossible.

Ordinary Borderlanders, those with no magic, had always known of the Shadow Cartographers and those who followed the dark path. It had been a minor part of life, but now, bands of mutants roamed the land, taking women and girls back to the Fertility Halls, increasingly spread across multiple locations. Those who protested, who went to try to get their wives or daughters or sisters back, were taken to Elf, the silver-haired banshee Finn had seen stalking the plague field that night. Her magical ability was like a battery, draining, storing and transforming life energy. It was said that those who faced her were dragged away afterward as a husk of skin and bone, mouths open in a last terrible scream.

Finn turned the last corner into a dirt street a few blocks back from the central slave market. The stench of fish hung in the air from the drying racks nearby, a staple food for those in the trader town, but even that was under threat now. The closing of the border had impacted the giant shoals of herring that once darted through the porous line between the worlds. Nature was out of balance and Finn was sure that those on Earthside must be suffering, too. He could only hope that Sienna was okay.

He ducked between rows of huts and stood for a moment watching the area, alert for any who might track the Resistance. A dirty tarpaulin flapped at the door of a nearby shack, drawing his eyes, but it was just the wind. Children played with a misshapen ball near a pile of rubbish, but they didn't even glance in his direction. Those who lived here learned to turn a blind eye almost as soon as they could walk. Better not to notice what went on in these streets.

Finn hurried to a ramshackle hut, pushed the wooden

door open and ducked inside. The point of a sharp blade against his throat stopped him, the cold metal tight against his skin.

A beat of silence, then the knife dropped.

"You're meant to whistle, you idiot." Titus O'Byrne stepped forward into the light, sandy curls tied roughly back from his face. "I could have cut your throat."

Finn smiled. "Just making sure you're staying vigilant." He walked further inside. The tiny shack was barely large enough for the two of them, both sizeable men used to more generous quarters. It smelled of yesterday's soup, old sweat and the reek of the open sewers only meters outside but it was only a place to lie low while they investigated the latest abhorrent attempt by the Shadow Cartographers to shape the destiny of the Borderlands.

Finn placed the vial gently on the wooden tabletop. "There were soldiers everywhere and this cost us most of the gold we had left. I hope it was enough to keep the man from betraying our location, but I can't be sure. We need to move on."

Titus bent to look at the vial, his blue eyes reflecting the hues of the liquid within. "It's worth it, brother. This might be the key."

Finn smiled at his words. They were brothers in the war against the Shadow, but no one could mistake them for blood relations. Finn's heritage was evident in his black skin and the regal bearing of an Ethiopian king. Titus was stocky and muscular, with the body of a boxer and a face to match, with mixed Irish and South African blood. They had served together several years ago in the Warlord's army, but Titus had deserted to join the Resistance in the wake of the atrocities against the refugees, many of whom he counted amongst his kin. Titus had knowledge of the mines and training in chemistry, primarily for warfare, and now he used his talents to fight against the Shadow. He was a brother in every way that mattered.

Titus ran a fingertip along the edge of the glass vial. "There's a midwife who lives on the other side of town near the soup kitchen. She helps women infected with this stuff. The ... babies they deliver." He shivered, as if shaking off a bad dream. "She keeps them hidden from the soldiers, but I'm not sure they're better off ..." His words trailed away.

Finn nodded. "We'll figure out an antidote. There has to be one. But first, we have to change locations. I know somewhere that might have what you need to analyze this." He put his hand on Titus's shoulder. "One step at a time."

They packed up their meager belongings, pulled cloaks around to hide their weapons and headed out into the night.

Finn led the way, cutting through narrow walkways between the shacks, navigating the warren of the shanty town on the outskirts. He had come this way many times, the makeshift city a perfect place to lie low.

Most people here were just passing through, forced on to work the mines or serve in the Warlord's army, others for the Fertility Halls, and still more to the farmlands. There were many mouths to feed in the Borderlands, many who went hungry and took handouts from the soldiers who controlled the food supply. The blue poison was an addictive liquid that the destitute begged for, that dulled their minds and took the edge off their hunger. It was added to food in the trader town and handed out on street corners, sometimes in exchange for pleasure quickly taken.

A giggle came from the shadows as they passed by. A young woman sat with her back against a dirt wall, filthy and stinking clothes stretched over a swollen belly. Maybe only a few weeks until she gave birth. She might have been pretty once, but now she looked ravaged, her skin taking on the hue of a corpse. Yet she smiled coquettishly, as if she wandered through fields of poppies without a care in the world.

"Take your pleasure for some blue, why don't you, boys?"

The sweet smell of something like marijuana hung in the

air but it was nothing so mundane as that form of escape. The blue drug was known by many names. Some even called it Liberation because those who took it were finally free from their enslavement, no longer caring about death — or those they left behind. The women who took it gave birth to mutants, many taken to the Castle of the Shadow, most never seen again.

Titus stopped and bent down to the young woman. He pulled half a loaf of bread from his pack and gave it to her. "Eat this. You'll feel better."

She looked confused, as if she hadn't seen real food in a long time and didn't know what to do with it. Then she tore at the bread with both hands, stuffing pieces quickly into her mouth. Titus turned away, his shoulders stooped as if he carried the weight of her suffering away, but Finn knew the young woman and her unborn child were already lost. They walked on through the streets, leaving her behind. One more life consumed by the Shadow.

Finn heard trickles of information from his Resistance sources, some undercover in the castle itself, risking their lives to reveal the truth. The blue drug twisted the genetics of the unborn, adding a dash of chaos into the mix so new mutations emerged. On Earthside, the numbers of those with magic dwindled, but here in the Borderlands, their numbers grew every day, cultivated as part of a new order dedicated to the dark plans of the Shadow Cartographers. The children were tested for their magic and many were found wanting. They were taken for sacrifice at the Tophet, or shoveled into the plague pits. Those with a touch of magic were siphoned, drained of what little they had. Finn had heard tales of the silver-haired Elf sapping newborns dry, leaving their tiny corpses as husks to blow away in the wind.

Finn's sister, Isabel, had died in the Castle of the Shadow, his baby niece lost to him when the traitor, Jari, had betrayed him in the hunt for the Map of Plagues. Titus, too, was driven by love to find an antidote to the blue, but Finn knew it went deeper for both of them. There were rumors that the drug was made in a camp by a lake out east and for the sake of all the sisters and daughters of the Borderlands, they were determined to find the source and destroy it.

The edge of the city soon bled into the desert, ever encroaching sand that claimed more dwellings by the day. Finn and Titus trudged out into the dunes, the way made harder as their feet sank down with every step. Far ahead, the stark lines of a ruined temple cut a line through the cliff at the base of an escarpment. As they drew closer, Finn remembered the last time he had come here — with Sienna and the Mapwalker team, on the way to the forgotten city of Alexandria and the library at its heart. But this time, the temple was a waypoint for a different reason and Finn could only hope that the sanctuary still held its long-forgotten treasure.

By the time Finn and Titus made it to the entrance of the ruined temple, clouds hid the face of the moon. Statues of the old gods stood in alcoves around the walls, some with faces smashed in by followers of Moloch, devourer of children, and others painted with curses in languages from foreign shores. Finn walked slowly to the stone altar, his footsteps echoing in the empty space. Dried garlands of marigolds and lilies bound with ivy hung from its edge, evidence of believers who still honored the lost religion. The temple might be empty now, but its power still lingered.

Finn knelt in front of the altar, holding his sword in front of him as he had knelt so long ago back when he entered his father's service as a soldier in the Shadow Guard. But now he pledged allegiance not to the half-moon, but to the people of the Borderlands, and to the Resistance. He prayed for guidance and for strength in the inevitable battle to come.

A minute later, Finn stood up, leaning on his sword with a scrape of metal on stone.

Titus emerged from the shadows. "We need to get out of here before dawn. Patrols come here all the time."

Finn nodded toward the back of the temple where stone steps led down into darkness. "This way."

He pulled a metal torch from a bracket on the wall. It had a small patch of oil left inside. Finn lit it and carried the flame down the stairs.

A ritual bathing pool filled the chamber below, empty of water except for a few brackish puddles. A mosaic of cavorting gods in faded colors hinted at the temple pleasures in earlier times, but now it was only a breeding ground for mosquitoes.

At the opposite end of the room, an arched doorway led into darkness topped with a carving of heaped bones.

Finn walked on, through the arch and down a spiral staircase into the halls of the dead below the temple. Torchlight flickered across alcoves in the walls, some with linen-wrapped desiccated corpses, others with piles of bones.

"Only the most powerful were buried down here," Finn said, his voice echoing through the chamber. "There is one who was buried with everything he worked on, so no one could continue his quest. Superstition keeps people away even now."

He stopped in front of a massive boulder roughly hewn into an oval shape and rolled in front of an opening. There were symbols carved into the rock — triangles of fire and water, the circle of the golden sun, and curved lines representing the metals of the alchemist.

In the center, a roughly carved skull, eyes of pitted rock that seemed to stare out from the abyss. A warning in every culture. Death lies within.

CHAPTER 4

THE DOOR TO THE Antiquities department of the Ministry of Maps was suitably ancient. Some said it was made of wood from the cedars of Lebanon that King Solomon spoke of in his Song of Songs. Others that it was hewn from the spars of Greek warships after the sack of Troy. Love and war, appropriate reminders of the inevitability of history. Zoe Saroyan pushed open the door and stepped into what had become her world in the last month.

She had transferred from the Ministry office attached to the British Library in London, a promotion of sorts since the corridors of Bath were hallowed ground and most ancient maps now rested here. Zoe could sense the difference in power. The earth almost throbbed with it, amplified by the magic of those who worked within. But it had been thrown off balance, wounded by the Borderlander attack. The fire destroyed so much, and now it was all hands on deck to restore what remained.

Zoe was early as usual, but there were a few familiar faces already working, heads bent over vellum, cloth or paper, all diligent in trying to trace the lines on the maps, some burned beyond recognition, others salvageable to those who knew their craft, both worldly and magical.

Her own magic was muddled, a touch of this and that, but

Zoe had found her life's work in restoration. She could lose herself in the maps, her light touch turning a broken thing into something those with real magic could travel through once more. She was a little in awe of the Blood Mapwalkers, those who could travel through maps, even create their own, whose very essence could transform the boundaries of the world. Her abilities seemed paltry in comparison, but she did what she could.

At the British Library, Zoe had been responsible for tracing the provenance of older maps, finding those with magic imbued within them so they could be separated from purely Earthside cartography. The collection held in excess of four million individual maps, and even with her touch of weaver magic, Zoe couldn't work fast enough. But she must have done something right because now she was here, in the Ministry at Bath, part of the Antiquities team drafted in to help Restoration after the fire.

Each of the workers had a private area shielded by high panels so they could work in the way that best suited their gifts. Magic had a hierarchy, just as any part of society, and the Mapwalkers were no different. Blood Mapwalkers were the most revered — but they also took the most risk, and when they died, their skin became the maps that others traveled in their turn.

Below them were those with strong fire or water magic, and then those with other kinds of gifts, many of whom found their way to the Ministry over time. Zoe had heard a rumor that those in the Borderlands deliberately bred children of mixed magic, trying to encourage new forms to emerge. But here on Earthside, such things were forbidden and Zoe's own gift was considered a lesser form. But she could still be useful in her quiet way, and to be honest, she was perfectly happy here in the quiet of Antiquities. She could dampen down the desire for something more — at least, most of the time.

Zoe primarily worked with the tools of every map restorer. De-acidification and removal of caustic adhesives from incorrect backing materials. Preparation and flattening, bleaching and cleaning, cutting where necessary, re-backing with linen. But she specialized in fixing rips and tears both physical and magical, and she suspected that this was why she had been asked to come to Bath.

She circled behind her desk, placing her bag underneath as she looked down at the map pinned gently to the surface. The Egyptian papyrus depicted a fifteen-kilometer stretch of Wadi Hammamat in the Eastern Desert made for Pharaoh Ramesses IV on a quarrying expedition. Although initially thought to show only rock formations, a magical imprint had been overlaid in generations past, now disturbed by the degradation of the map. Unless it was restored, the ancient paths would be lost forever. Zoe had studied Egyptology and ancient Egyptian hieroglyphics as part of her degree. If she could restore the papyrus, perhaps she could also restore the Mapwalker magic that lay interwoven with its strands.

She walked to the coffee machine in the corner, a filter system that seemed as ancient as the room itself. She poured herself a generous mug and went back to her desk. In the last few days, she had been preparing the map in traditional ways as she had learned in her degree in Conservation and Restoration from Lincoln University, home to the largest center for such work in the UK. She had already placed re-moistenable repair paper over the worst of the cracks. It was made from high-grade Japanese paper coated with a cellulose gum that would not degrade the papyrus, one of the best ways to both protect what was left and repair the map. But as Zoe looked down at the lines depicting the Wadi, she knew she had done everything traditionally possible as a restorer. It was time to move to the next step.

Her white gloves lay next to the map, and usually, reaching for them was her first task of the day. But now she left them to the side and concentrated on the map itself. Zoe softened her gaze into the space above the lines and curves and colors of ancient Egypt. As her focus shifted, contours appeared in the air, suspended as if woven from motes of dust and glimmers of sunlight. Tears and fissures cracked through the dimensions, breaking the perfection of the original magical lines and weakening its fabric.

Zoe raised her hands and began to gently tease the contours back into shape, weaving the magic together as if she stitched an intricate pattern in the air. The room fell away around her as she concentrated, barely breathing as she sensed the holes and gaps and filled them with little drops of her gift.

As the minutes passed, she began to comprehend the unseen undulations of the magical map. She had worked on enough of these multi-layered papyri to learn the conventions of how early Mapwalkers structured their cartography, but this one was different. Zoe frowned as she considered a particular layer over the quarry. As much as she tried to weave the contours together, it resisted her magic; the tendrils coming undone even as she repeated her actions. It was strange, something she had never encountered before, but she was sure her mother would have.

Her mother's family had been Christian refugees from Armenia, fleeing the Ottoman Empire in the wake of genocide. Three generations had passed but the pain of persecution and the loss of their homeland persisted, a shared legacy that permeated songs and stories told over and over to keep the memory alive.

Many of the women of her mother's bloodline had been renowned weavers — both of cloth and of magic. Her father was a British accountant, a straight-backed man of impeccable manners, a port in the emotional storm that was her mother's intensity. Zoe was their only child, and whenever she went home to the terraced house in Clapham, south

London, they wanted to know everything, all the details of her life. She left London partly to escape their constrictive orbit, but her mother had taught her everything about weaving, and she could use the help now.

Zoe took a deep breath. She did not want to call her mother and explain why she needed help. She had left London for a reason, and she could work this out herself. She just needed to go back to first principles.

The first step in untangling a bad weave was to step back and look at it from a fresh angle, to try and work out what could be released elsewhere to free tension from the knots. Brute strength made a tangle worse, whereas gentle easing could solve the problem and leave the strands unbroken. Zoe took a step backward to shift her perspective on the contours that hung in the air. But there was nothing new to see, and she bit her lip in frustration.

She hunkered down, squatting on the ground to look up from below and there, suddenly, she saw it. A golden thread hung from the underside of the deep quarry lines, a shimmering cord of magic that implied … another layer.

Zoe couldn't help the gasp that escaped her lips at the realization. She had read so many maps where there was only one layer of magic woven into the threads; she had never considered that there might be more below that. She reached for the golden thread and as she touched it, a jolt of energy passed through her. The scent of sandalwood filled the air and as she caressed the length of cord, she saw another dimension, another layer of magic, woven beneath the first.

She blinked, shaking her head a little, trying to adjust her focus so she could see what lay below. But it was as if she had only stitched a tiny part of the whole and much was left to be revealed. Perhaps fixing the upper layer further would uncover more.

Zoe stood again and worked faster, her fingers darting

in and out of silver contours, motes of light dancing around her as stitch by stitch, she remade the map.

It seemed as if time slowed while Zoe dwelled within and between the layers, fingers flashing faster, a smile playing around her lips. For so long, she had held her weaver magic in check, not daring to use it much for fear of discovery amongst those who knew not of Mapwalkers, but also for fear of the drops of shadow that all exchanged for the use of their gift. But now, Zoe glimpsed the possibilities. How many more maps had these layers, hidden magical paths below what was obvious? What else could she discover?

She made the final stitch in the upper layer of magic and the Egyptian papyrus seemed renewed, at least through her eyes. The physical cracks disappeared as the magical ones closed, and then it was as if the entire thing became a three-dimensional puzzle. She bent down to look on the underside, her eyes sparkling at what lay below outlined in threads of golden light.

Zoe carefully examined the network of underground caverns. What had been a plain quarry on the surface was clearly a funerary complex of great riches, a hidden treasure trove undiscovered by Egyptologists. An area of barren desert may well harbor the greatest wealth.

She traced a path through the chambers, glimpsing golden hieroglyphics on the walls, woven into the magical fabric. She frowned as she recognized symbols from the Book of the Dead, markers on the path to the afterlife.

Warnings and curses. A forbidden place.

What could possibly be down there that needed so much protection?

CHAPTER 5

Sienna stepped into the library, a bag over her shoulder containing her grandfather's journal. She stood in the doorway for a moment, gazing around at what was left. The fire had carved a swathe through the dry paper and ancient vellum once stacked on the English oak shelves that now stood bowed and blackened — but not completely ravaged. Perhaps nothing could really destroy the heart of the Ministry.

A rustle came from deeper within the room.

Sienna walked further in and rounded the shelves to the annex where once the Illuminated Cartographer could be found at study. At first glance, it was as if nothing had changed.

The area had been partially protected by the sheer density of maps and more had been brought from other departments to replace them. Rolled sheets of vellum painted with routes to distant places lined the walls. Tiny fragments of papyrus lay pinned within frames next to a grand print of an ancient sea map with a tentacled monster nestled in one corner. Glimpses of what it had once been — but the smell of burned paper still hung in the air, a reminder of recent desolation.

A figure stood at a desk piled high with books and for

a moment, Sienna thought she saw the craggy features of the Illuminated emerging from the maps. She blinked, and the image faded as Bridget turned. Her close-cropped dark hair still curled around fine features and piercing blue eyes. She still had laughter lines and an air of mischief, but it was tempered now with a darker stain, and her shoulders hung heavy as if she bore a great weight upon them. Where once she had worn multi-colored dresses of patchwork stitching, she now clothed herself in maps. They wound about her, wrapping her body in layers of lines and symbols, overlaying the tattoos she had etched on her skin. At her wrists, ink merged with blood, a pulsing of life and magic that sustained the border at a cost beyond imagining.

"Did we do the right thing when we closed the border?" Sienna said softly.

"We did what we could." Bridget shrugged, the maps rustling around her at the movement. "But I still don't know. It's impossible to tell." She turned back to the desk, indicating the books stacked high around her. "The reports of natural disasters keep coming, and the annals of the Mapwalkers have little of help. This has never been done before."

Sienna walked to the desk and touched the leather spine of one book. Words of those long dead meant nothing as people continued to die every day in the here and now.

"You can open the border again though, right?"

Bridget sighed. "It's hard to tell. When my blood mingled with the maps that day, I used significant power to close it. It would take much more to reverse that action." She hung her head. "I don't know if I can do it alone, or if I have the strength to maintain it without letting in a tide of Borderlanders."

Sienna put a hand out to touch the edge of the maps that curled around Bridget's arm. "You're not alone. There are still Blood Mapwalkers who stand alongside you, those who will fight for Earthside."

Bridget turned her palms upward and Sienna looked

down to see where the maps entered her veins at the wrists. Her blood turned to a deep indigo — not the dark blue of the Shadow but more the cobalt of Chinese porcelain or the hood of a saint in the stained glass of a medieval cathedral.

"You can still walk away," Bridget said. "It's too late for me. I decided to give my life For Galileo a long time ago, but you have a chance to get away from here."

Sienna took Bridget's hand in her own. She could feel the blood and ink pulsing between them and something called to the magic within her. Like calling to like. "This is my life now, too. I had no direction before coming here, no idea why I felt so restless. Now I know my place in this world and the one beyond." For a moment, Sienna hesitated, unsure of the next step. She bit her lip and then sighed. "But there is something I need to show you."

She pulled up her t-shirt with her other hand, revealing the whorls of shadow that patterned her torso.

Bridget gasped, her eyes widening. She dropped Sienna's hand in shock, the connection of ink and blood severed once more. "How did it happen?"

Sienna shook her head. "I don't know exactly. It ebbs and flows as I use my magic, but something is different now. I think I might be able to sustain a balance of shadow."

Bridget bent to look at the patterns more closely. "I've never seen marks as dense as this on someone still functioning. You have to see one of the doctors—"

"But—"

Bridget held up a hand. "Don't even try to argue. You'll see Dr Rachel Tabib. She's younger than most of the other Ministry doctors, more open-minded about possibilities. Please, Sienna. Your father will be so worried."

Sienna nodded. "Alright, but just to ease his mind. I'm not being confined to some ward while I have time left to find this." She opened the bag and pulled out her grandfather's journal.

Bridget moved a heavy tome to one side and Sienna glimpsed a figure sketched in black lines spinning in a vortex of shadow and blood on its ivory pages.

"Show me," Bridget said.

Sienna placed the journal on the desk and opened it to a page marked with a purple silk ribbon. Intricate drawings covered the paper, sketches of giant stones at the base of a pyramid, a boy lounging against a palm tree eating dates next to a sleeping camel, the triangular sail of a felucca on the waters of the Nile beyond.

Bridget bent to look closer. "Michael traveled often to Egypt on Earthside when he worked with the Antiquities department. Sometimes he would cross over to the Borderlands to fetch artifacts pushed over in ancient times. Why do you think this is unusual?"

Sienna turned the page. "He sketched a lot of tombs and because he saw so many, he noted when they were different, when they stood out somehow." She pointed to a set of hieroglyphics and the scrawled handwriting underneath. *Map of the Impossible.*

Sienna flicked through the subsequent pages. "Look here and here. He found these marks in several tombs but never discovered what it referred to. They were all etched with funerary texts and paths through the underworld to the land beyond."

Bridget traced the lines with a gentle fingertip. "You think the land beyond might be the Borderlands?"

"It's possible. We have to at least consider it as an option."

Bridget nodded. "Even if I could open the border once more, it would allow the invasion of the Shadow Cartographers and the forces of the Warlord. The best option is for you and the Mapwalker team to find another way through and see if you can work with the Resistance to change things over there before we open it again."

"We need someone who knows hieroglyphics with us."

The sound of hurried footsteps came from outside, then the door to the library banged open.

John rushed in, his face etched with concern as he rounded the corner of the annex. "You both have to see this."

He carried a tablet computer with the news playing on mute. He turned it to face Sienna and Bridget as he switched on the sound.

"The evacuation of San Francisco is continuing under almost impossible conditions this morning as earthquakes intensify. Emergency sirens sound throughout the downtown area and residents have been asked to calmly leave as fast as possible."

John muted the sound again even as horrific images of the aftermath of the Pacific Island disaster played on the screen, followed by footage of cars streaming east away from the coast of California, people running from what was on its way. The news cut to photographs from the 1906 earthquake that devastated San Francisco. Thousands of people dead, buildings destroyed and hundreds of thousands left homeless. Images of the stricken city seared on the memory of those who thought this day would never come in their lifetime.

"We could not have foreseen the impact of closing the border," John said. "But more people will die from natural disasters than might have died from invasion or the plague if we don't get it open again. We're running out of time."

* * *

Zoe felt a touch on her shoulder. She jumped, the vision of the golden underworld dropping away, the veil of magic dissipating as her focus shifted.

The Head of the Antiquities department stood by her side, the woman's gnomish face crinkled in curiosity. "Found something interesting?" She bent to look more closely at the map on the desk.

Her words made Zoe hesitate. She didn't really know what she'd found, but she didn't want to share anything yet. Not until she was sure.

"Perhaps, but I need more time."

"Well, you won't have it today. You're needed in the library."

Zoe's heart beat faster at the prospect of going to the center of the Ministry, the soul of the maps. She had visited the place briefly when she arrived as part of her induction tour, but it was a mess of charred ruins and everyone had ignored her, consumed as they were by cleanup tasks. She could only hope it was better now.

"What for?"

"Something Egyptian, right up your alley. Get going. Don't keep the Illuminated waiting."

Zoe grabbed her notebook and pen, as much for something to clutch onto as anything else, something to anchor her hammering heart.

She hurried through the corridors of the Ministry, winding her way toward the library. Thoughts ran through her mind, possibilities about how she could help. Perhaps she might become an important part of the team, or maybe she would just disappoint them and have to leave Bath almost as soon as she had arrived, slinking back to her parents in shame and failure. This was such an important moment in her career. She couldn't mess it up. But what if she did?

With her mind teeming, Zoe paused at the doorway to the library and took a deep breath. There was only one way to discover what came next. She stepped inside.

Rolled maps lined the walls of the first chamber alongside what was left of the ancient books that had survived the fire. A large framed photo took pride of place near the door, an image of what the library had been only months before — and what might be again with time and care.

"Come on through."

The voice came from the other side of the shelving and Zoe rounded the end to find herself in a smaller annex. This was much cozier than the grand entrance, clearly where the Illuminated worked. The woman clothed in maps turned around. She was beautiful in the way of the Pre-Raphaelite painters, women of ivory skin frozen in time, captured in the moment before their inevitable death. Something about her made Zoe want to curtsey.

"Welcome." The Illuminated stepped forward, maps rustling around her as she held out a hand. "I'm Bridget. This is Sienna and John."

Zoe shook Bridget's hand, shocked into silence. She stood with those considered royalty amongst the Mapwalkers. John Farren was a legend of many explorations and the Antiquities department had much he had collected on his travels. He was marked by scars, bowed with the pain of torture, but his eyes were still a steely blue.

Sienna's reputation was new, an estranged daughter who turned out to be far more than expected, with powerful blood magic that both empowered the Mapwalkers and endangered their future. Many within the Ministry considered her arrogant, given too much responsibility before she was ready purely because of her heritage. But Zoe saw doubt in Sienna's eyes, a fragility she had not expected. There was also a palpable sense of misgiving in the room.

"Hi, thanks for inviting me over." Zoe cursed the words almost as soon as they were out. She needed something better to impress the magical elite.

"We're hoping you can help us." Sienna pointed to the desk.

An old book lay to one side with a figure sketched in ash on its ivory pages, turning in a vortex of shadow and light. Next to it, a journal open to a page of hieroglyphics etched between the lines of a hand-drawn sketch.

Zoe found herself drawn closer, her love of Egyptology quashing the nerves that skittered through her veins. She bent to the page and examined the finely drawn images, translating the symbols in her mind. They were well-known passages from the Book of the Dead, and time slowed as she let the words wash over her.

She turned the page and a scent of cedar wood rose as if she were with the man who wrote these words, copying them from the walls of a chill tomb surrounded by the dust of the long dead. These were no common symbols. They were reflections of what she had seen in the golden layer of Wadi Hammamat. Zoe couldn't help the gasp that escaped her lips.

"What is it?" Bridget came closer as the others gathered round. "What do you see?"

Zoe pointed to a set of glyphs on the page. "These symbols are incredibly rare, a form of Mapwalker magic used to place maps within maps within maps."

John frowned. "A third layer of cartography? I've heard rumors of this, but I've met no one who could make or decipher them. A bloodline lost in the genocide of the east, perhaps."

His words echoed through Zoe, a call to her ancestral past. "My mother's family are from Armenia originally. We're Weavers."

"Weavers?" Sienna sounded curious. "You mean you weave cloth?"

"And magic," Bridget said, her eyes piercing as she looked at Zoe with new interest. "Weavers can layer objects with a magical thread and some can even manipulate the cords of the world." She placed a hand on Zoe's arm. "Where have you seen these glyphs before?"

Her touch was gentle, encouraging, but Zoe also felt an edge in the hard lines of the maps that encased her body. There was only one authority here.

"I'm restoring a map down in Antiquities. On one plane, it's an ancient quarry, but as I stitched, I found a layer below, that of a treasure house hidden under the rock. Then I found a golden thread to a third layer, a set of tombs. This glyph marks the door implying it is a way through the border in the realm between the living and the dead. There is no exact translation that I can find, but it means something like 'impossible.'" Zoe pointed to the journal. "This person knew something of Egyptology to translate such a word. Perhaps he was in the tomb, perhaps he found a way inside."

"Could you find such a place if you were in that quarry?" John asked. His words made Zoe's heart beat faster again. Something within her wanted this so very much.

"I don't know. Perhaps." She whispered the last word, like a prayer.

Bridget nodded. "Sienna, get Perry and Mila down here. You'll go together with Zoe, find these golden chambers, and see if the Map of the Impossible leads you to the Borderlands. In the meantime, John and I will continue searching for answers."

A decision made, a page turned, a life changed.

Zoe took a deep breath. She was ready.

CHAPTER 6

Titus couldn't tear his eyes away from the skull. It was clearly a warning, but death had already come for the people of the Borderlands and they had little left to lose.

Finn put the torch into a metal bracket on one side. "Help me move this."

Together, they put their shoulders against the rock and with a scrape of stone; they pushed it aside.

The tomb was hacked into the mountain itself, each cut made by hand to honor one so greatly revered. A stone sarcophagus stood in the center, adorned with alchemical symbols and around the casket, the implements and tools of the alchemist himself.

Titus took a deep breath as he gazed around at the tomb. It smelled musty with a metallic edge, like dried blood on a sword after battle. Thick benches of black wood lined the walls, piled with brass implements mottled with age. Bottles of varying sizes stoppered with beeswax lay in boxes, thrown together hastily in a mosaic of colored glass each containing mysterious liquid or powder. If only they had more time. He could spend a generation studying what lay here.

"Who was this guy?"

Finn ran a fingertip across the top of the sarcophagus, tracing lines in the dust. "Some accounts say it's Nicolas

Flamel, a fifteenth-century scribe and seller of rare manuscripts who discovered the philosopher's stone. It is said that two hundred years after his death, he learned the steps to immortality from a *converso* on the road to Santiago, a pilgrimage town on Earthside." He shrugged. "Clearly, it didn't help him much. His corpse still lies here. But this place has been used by other chemists over time, so perhaps something lies here for you now."

Titus hunkered down by one of the boxes, his eye caught by spidery writing on the labels. Hemlock, deadly nightshade, snakeroot and rosary pea. All deadly poisons in the right dosage. Sometimes, the same compound could be used in small measure for the good of the patient and where there was poison, there was often an antidote.

The alchemical symbols covering the central stone sarcophagus brought back memories of studying books in the Warlord's forbidden library back in Old Aleppo. He would creep in at night to read after a day of hard training and no matter how tired he was, Titus always made time to learn. He was muscular and physically powerful, even as a teenager, so it was assumed he was more brawn than brains. But his mother encouraged him to read from an early age and above all, Titus valued knowledge.

When the Warlord caught him one night with a chemistry book and tested him on his knowledge, Kosai directed him into munitions, helping to research new compounds for war. But Titus had learned enough to understand the balance in nature — that what can destroy can sometimes heal, and perhaps that applied to people as well as plants. After he joined the Resistance, he swore that he would only use his knowledge to help the people of the Borderlands from then on.

Titus knew that the drug Liberation had a natural plant base, grown in vast fields on the plains out east. Perhaps lupine or locoweed, known to cause birth defects in animals, but not strong enough to bring on miscarriage. It was mutated with magic, imbued with something that encouraged the genetic makeup of the fetus to develop new powers, some never seen before. Every day it was used in the population meant more children born under the veil of shadow.

Enough. He would not let it continue any longer.

Titus turned to Finn. "We need a still. Look for glass flasks of different sizes." He pointed to the benches and boxes on the far side. "Search those — but be gentle. This stuff is fragile and you don't want to break open one of those bottles. Who knows what we might breathe in?"

Finn hunted through the boxes, and Titus searched his side of the room. He needed to distill the liquid down to understand what it was made of. Perhaps that way he might discover some method to neutralize it. But of course, that would only reverse the natural element of the drug. The magical part could only be stopped by destroying the manufacturing plant. Perhaps his munitions expertise might come in handy, after all.

He pulled out another box and picked through the vials, carefully examining each before laying them gently aside. His fingers were soon covered in the dust of years, but he kept going at a steady pace. As every minute passed, time ticked away for his wife and the baby that grew inside her.

Maria had trained alongside him in the Shadow Guards, a lithe athlete with a ready laugh who pulled him out of the library on sunny days to dance in the water fountains and make love in the dappled olive groves. But he had not known that the women of the guards were encouraged to take Liberation, and if they rejected the drug, it was dosed in their food, anyway. When Maria found herself pregnant, they rejoiced — until the moment she found herself craving the drug, then demanding it, a slave to the blue addiction. That's when Titus had turned to the Resistance for help.

Now Maria lay tied to a bed in the rebel base in the

mountains, screaming as she went through never-ending withdrawal, her mind lost to the drug. The child growing within would likely be mutated and if discovered, it would be sent for evaluation. The Resistance camps were full of such children now, born in secret, some physically altered, others with anomalous abilities, others still completely normal — or so it seemed.

If Titus could find an antidote for Maria in time, maybe their child would be one of the lucky ones. He could only do what lay within his power — and he knew chemistry. He could not hide in the mountains listening to her scream when his action might save her and so many others.

"Is this it?" Finn's voice broke into his thoughts and Titus spun around.

Finn held a glass alembic, an alchemical still made from two glass vessels connected by a downward-sloping tube. It was dusty, but it would be enough.

Titus cleared a space on the bench top. "Put it here, gently now." Finn placed it down with care and wiped the glass with the edge of his shirt.

Titus searched in the same box and found an iron tripod, dulled to a dusty grey, to hold the alembic above a flame. He set up the equipment, part of him wishing he had lived in the mysterious time when the alchemists searched for the secrets of transformation. In another life, perhaps Titus could have joined the search for the philosopher's stone or the perilous route to immortality. For alchemists did not merely seek to turn base metal to gold. That was mere camouflage for their real mission, the true metamorphosis of nature itself.

With the alembic in place, Titus poured the blue liquid inside, hoping that whatever had been in it last was long evaporated and would not contaminate the sample. Finn lit the tiny pool of oil underneath the flask and within seconds, it began to bubble.

The first drop of liquid appeared at the top of the connecting pipe and slid down into the receiving beaker, with another following. Titus caught the next on his fingertip, its color now faint blue, like the reflection of water in ice. He sniffed it first — only a slight hint of sweetness, like honeysuckle in a far-off hedgerow. He touched a tiny amount to his tongue, closed his eyes and concentrated on the sensation. Chemists down the ages had relied on this most basic of tests and there was no time for anything much more sophisticated right now.

A definite sweetness followed by a dry mouth, his heart beating faster almost immediately. Signs of one of the most deadly plants, easily grown in terrains throughout the Borderlands. Laced with magic, certainly, but the base was a common noxious weed. Titus opened his eyes.

"It's mostly belladonna, sometimes called deadly nightshade. I'm sure of it. The antidote can be extracted from the seeds of the Calabar bean, which in itself is a poison, so it must be used carefully. The alchemist must have had some." He searched the bench, rifling through bottles of multi-hued powders.

Finn investigated the opposite side of the tomb. "What does it look like?"

"Black, small like a coffee bean. Maybe ground powder or perhaps in pods about six inches long."

After a few minutes, Titus unearthed an ebony box and opened the lid to find a black powder inside. A hand-written label pasted on the inside noted the danger of the Calabar. "Found it."

"How do we know it will work?" Finn asked.

Titus sighed. "We can't know for sure. The only way is to take it back to the trader town and test it. The midwife I know is ready to try anything to save the women and children in her care. She'll help us."

Titus held the box in his hand, knowing that the powder

was just as much a poison as Liberation itself. But in the chemistry of plants, this was often true. Dosage was everything and what could save one might kill another.

It was a step in the right direction and he had to do something practical or he would go crazy with thoughts of Maria's torment. Every night he dreamed of mutated babies thrown into blood pits at the Castle of the Shadow, their tiny faces contorted in screams. Action was the only way he knew how to deal with it all — and he would keep going until Liberation was ended, or until he was.

"Check the boxes for any more of it," Titus said. "And anything labeled with Manchineel. But whatever you do, don't get it on your skin. In tiny doses, Manchineel can counteract belladonna, but it is one of the most toxic plants, known as the little apple of death."

Finn gave a rueful smile. "And I thought my sword was the best weapon."

After an inch by inch search of the place, they collected up five boxes of powder, three of Calabar and two of Manchineel. Titus wrapped them carefully with lengths of rag found in piles beneath the benches so the boxes wouldn't leak and then loaded them carefully into backpacks.

At the door to the tomb, he looked back at the cornucopia of alchemy. He could only hope to amass such a heritage by the time he left this earth. Perhaps there would be time after they had ended the Liberation addiction for him to pursue the knowledge he craved. But not today.

Together, Finn and Titus rolled back the stone and left the ruined temple. As they hiked back through the desert, energy renewed by their find, Titus outlined his plan.

"This will be enough for initial tests in the trader town. Once we know what works, we can source more antidote ingredients. They're tropical plants, so we'd need to go inland."

Finn nodded. "I know of such a place where we might

find them. It has giant beasts and the produce of the rainforest might be just as bountiful."

"We can send a team out there to find more." Titus couldn't help the grin on his face, encouraged by their find and its potential. "While you manage that, I'll take a tiny batch to the mountains for Maria. She'll be well again, the baby will be perfect. This will work, Finn, I know it."

As they walked on through the night, Titus thought three steps ahead, planning the mechanism by which they might harvest the drugs, how long it might take to produce a batch of antidote, and how they could get it to the farthest reaches of the Borderlands. He carried hope on his back and for now, that was enough.

CHAPTER 7

Sienna couldn't have walked much more slowly to the door of the medical wing of the Ministry, but since Bridget wouldn't let her leave with the team until a doctor had cleared her, she forced herself to go. She tried to think of it as a positive step, valuable preparation before what could be an arduous journey, but her limbs were heavy as if her very being rejected the idea of such help.

Like all the doors of the Ministry, this one was solid wood. A dark grained ebony embedded with a carved Rod of Asclepius, a serpent entwined around a staff, representing the Greek god of healing and medicine. The rod was made from willow bark, used in many cultures as a pain reliever. All of this should have made Sienna feel better, but a sense of foreboding rose inside as she raised a hand to push at the door. There were stories of those who entered here and never emerged again. But there was nothing she could do but face whatever would come. She braced herself and walked inside.

The ancient wooden door disguised ultra-modern facilities within. A waiting room with comfy chairs decorated in shades of sage green, the relaxing scent of lavender. But underneath the calm, Sienna could make out the beep of medical devices in the ward beyond and the smell of antiseptic that betrayed the true nature of this place.

Her pulse raced at the possibility of being trapped here. She would not be entombed in the bowels of the earth. She turned to duck back out the door.

"Welcome!" The voice was warm and sweet, like peppermint tea served to guests as hospitality. An open gesture that promised no harm.

Sienna stopped, took a deep breath and turned round.

Dr Rachel Tabib was rounded and bespectacled, short and plump with a wide smile. Her straight dark hair was tied back in a no-nonsense ponytail and her Middle Eastern origins were clear in her darker skin and slight accent.

Rachel smiled. "Were you leaving?"

A beat of silence as Sienna considered her options. She could leave now, avoid all of this. Would Bridget really stop her from traveling to the Borderlands? She might want to, but Sienna knew her magic was necessary, so she'd probably be allowed to go, anyway.

But as she looked into Rachel's eyes, she sensed no threat, only gentleness and a desire to help. There was almost a hum of healing magic around the doctor, as if she had a hive of golden bees inside, producing honey to soothe those in need.

Sienna shook her head. "I'm staying."

Rachel indicated an open door behind her. "Please come this way."

The smell of antiseptic grew stronger as they walked together down a corridor to a suite of examination rooms. A nurse walked past and glanced down at Sienna's arms, his eyes widening in concern. Sienna pulled the sleeves of her t-shirt down, covering the tendrils of black that grew more intense as her anxiety rose. She tried to dampen them down, breathing deeply to calm her fear. The Shadow fed on such emotion and she could only keep it in check if she controlled herself.

Once inside the examination room, Rachel closed the door. "I saw what you did out there. Can I see your arms now?"

Sienna pulled up her sleeves again to reveal the marks already fading to grey.

Rachel reached out a hand. "May I?"

Sienna nodded.

The doctor's touch was feather light as she traced the whorls, her gaze following the patterns. "I've never seen them fade so quickly."

"I have more." Sienna's voice wavered a little, and she felt the prick of tears. She realized how much concern she had been holding inside and how worried she really was about the marks.

Rachel stepped back and Sienna pulled off her t-shirt to stand in her bra. Her skin prickled in the cool air and she was acutely aware that she must look diseased or infected. Tainted by darkness.

But the doctor's eyes brightened. "They're beautiful, Sienna. Truly, I've never seen anyone like this, not here in the wards or in any of the Ministry records."

"What is it usually like?"

Rachel sighed and shook her head, as if seeing the faces of lost patients before her. "The Shadow usually presents as a stain through the blood and blooms on the skin like a bruise. Once it reaches a certain point, the individual is overwhelmed and slips into a coma of nightmares."

Sienna remembered the horror of the shadow weave and felt her chest constrict. The whorls darkened and swirled across her skin, moving like constellations, their power held in check until an inevitable explosive end. They spun faster, obscuring the freckles on her pale skin.

Rachel reached behind her to press the emergency call button, her eyes wide with panic.

"Wait," Sienna said. She closed her eyes and thought of her grandfather's map shop, the rustle of paper like stalks of corn in a summer field edged with poppies, the smell of elderflower as she walked along the canal and the sound of birdsong. As her breath returned to an even cadence, tension releasing from her body, she sensed the marks fade. She opened her eyes.

Rachel stood in stunned silence. "You can control it?"

Sienna nodded. "I think so. I just don't know how much I can take, or how long I could do it for, or under what conditions. I have so many questions and no one to talk to."

Rachel held out a hand and took Sienna's. "You can talk to me, but I can't possibly understand what you're going through. Nobody can."

Sienna pulled her long-sleeved t-shirt back on. "I don't want Bridget or my father to know how extensive this is. They'll stop me going to the Borderlands again."

"They want to protect you."

Sienna nodded. "Yes, but I need to discover what this means. Something draws me back there. I have dreams …"

Rachel froze. "Dreams?"

"Of the Tower of the Winds, voices calling my name. I'm flying with creatures who might tear me apart, but I long to soar with them between the worlds."

"That's more like the reports of those who slip into shadow coma. They talk of being called over there, of desperately wanting to go. Be careful, Sienna, the Shadow is not always what it seems."

"What could happen to me?" Sienna asked softly.

Rachel met her gaze without flinching. "Come to the ward. See for yourself."

Without waiting for a reply, Rachel walked to the door, and a second later, Sienna followed. Behind the examination rooms, there was another row of doors. Like much of the Ministry below the streets of Bath, it extended in unexpected directions. Sienna suspected magical layers to the geography as it was impossible to see how there was space for everything down here.

Rachel pushed open one of the doors to a darkened space

beyond, lit only by occasional lamps that cast golden pools of light onto faces of sleeping patients. She beckoned and together they stepped onto the ward, walking softly between the beds.

It was calm and quiet and for a moment, Sienna wondered why there were such dire stories about the place. The patients looked well cared for and at peace. Then she noticed the black lines running under their skin, the marks of shadow holding them in a netherworld from which they could not escape.

A moan came from one of the beds.

Monitors beeped faster and a distant alarm sounded from outside the ward. The sound of running footsteps.

A young woman thrashed against her padded shackles, terrified of something in her nightmare. She howled, an animal sound from the core of what remained of her humanity, the part of her that could still respond. The lines of her IV drip stretched as she arched her body off the mattress, straining to escape her bonds.

Sienna wanted to run, but she couldn't tear her eyes away. Thoughts of the shadow weave that Sir Douglas had trapped her in surfaced once more, memories of teeth and claws that ripped into soft flesh, devouring what was left of her. To be trapped in something like that was beyond terrible.

The nurse they had passed earlier jogged in, his concentration fixed on the patient. He nodded briefly at Rachel, then went to the woman's side. He pressed a button to increase the dose of sedative and after a moment, the terrified woman lapsed back into fitful unconsciousness. But her mouth still twisted in pain, her fingers clutching at the sheets.

"Can't you help her?" Sienna whispered. "She's still in distress."

Rachel shook her head. "We've tried so many things and continue to experiment with more. But the coma is powerful, and the Shadow has its hooks in deep. Each of these Mapwalkers invited it in, a drop for every use of magic. You know the dangers, Sienna, and even though you have some ability to control it, who knows where that may lead. The only way to wake these people up is to take them into the Borderlands."

"So why keep them here?"

Rachel frowned. "What would happen to them over there? Slaughtered by the Warlord, sucked dry of their magic in one of the dark chambers, or turned into Shadow Cartographers like Sir Douglas Mercator — perhaps the deepest cut of all. I have heard of what goes on over there."

"But there is also beauty, and good people fighting in the Resistance — and hope for a different future." Sienna walked over to the bed and looked down at the young woman, her body and mind ravaged by a nightmare. "Perhaps even a way to end all this."

Rachel came to stand next to her. "If you think there is a chance, I won't stop you — I'll tell Bridget you have time left before the stain is critical — but you have to understand the danger, Sienna. I don't want to see you in one of these beds."

* * *

As dawn turned the sky coral-pink, Titus and Finn reached the outskirts of the trader town. Early morning workers emerged from the doors of the shanty-town huts, eyes blearily assessing the strangers before turning away.

Titus led the way, weaving through narrow lanes until they reached the densely populated center of town. Larger buildings made of stone and brick lined these streets, designed to last longer than the outer camp dwellings. Wealthy merchants lived in the upper floors, a world away from the living conditions of those they enslaved. Their servants lived in warrens of underground rooms beneath.

Over the years, these basement dwellings had been sublet, knocked together and turned into enterprises for the working class. In one such subterranean cellar, deep down and heavily insulated, Kabila the midwife helped women give birth away from the prying eyes of the Shadow Guards, those who would take the babies or even the women themselves for the camps.

Titus paused at a small wooden hatch in the side of one house, more like a hurricane shelter than a proper door. He knocked once, twice, once again, then waited.

A minute later, the hatch opened slightly.

Kabila smiled up at him, the lines on her face deepening in a broad smile. "Come in, come in."

Titus clambered inside and Finn followed close behind, shutting the hatch behind him and bolting it securely.

Kabila walked ahead down a tunnel with a ceiling so low, both Titus and Finn had to bend down. The midwife was short and wide with ample curves draped in a faded red sari embroidered with silver thread, a remnant of her Indian heritage.

She had told Titus about her early memories one night as they sat waiting for the guards to pass by overhead, how she had been aboard one of the refugee boats escaping a flood. Her family had found themselves lost in the dark and woken to find themselves in the Borderlands. Titus would never forget the look on her face as she recounted the terror of being torn from her mother's arms, from seeing her father beaten to the ground, her older sister taken by the guards for the Fertility Halls.

Kabila had been sold as a child slave to the household of the wealthy merchant whose house she still lived beneath so many years later. When she had outlived her use for her master's pleasure, she worked in the kitchens, learning from women in the warrens all the ways she could help the girls of the trader town. Kabila had eventually taken on the mantle of underground midwife, while still maintaining her day job above ground. It was dangerous work. The soldiers of the Shadow would be only too happy to destroy the rebels helping women in trouble, but Kabila saw her lost sister in every young woman saved and she lived for the cause.

"Come and have tea." The midwife led them into a cozy kitchen with low stools around a small table. Everything down here was compact and basic, but somehow it felt welcoming and just as it should be. Titus glimpsed a room beyond with a simple bed over a stone floor, scrubbed clean of the blood shed in childbirth, but still bearing marks from the suffering within. He thought of Maria, tied to such a bed in the mountains, screaming his name. He shook his head to clear the image.

Kabila filled a rustic teapot with leaves and boiling water and let it steep on the table, steam rising from its spout in spirals. She placed cups down before it and then sat, hands folded in her lap, her eyes alive with curiosity.

"Now, tell me what you found."

Titus pulled the black boxes from the pack and explained what they had found in the alchemist's tomb.

"I'm sure the base of Liberation is made from belladonna. If we can try an antidote for that, perhaps the magic will not take in the womb."

As he explained the plan, Titus knew his words sounded farfetched. He saw doubt in Kabila's eyes. What had seemed possible under the moon faded away in the harsh light of day. His words trailed off …

Finn continued for him. "You could test these compounds and find the best option, then I can source more of these ingredients from the rainforest. We can make more of it. Send it all over the Borderlands. It's possible, isn't it?"

Kabila picked up the teapot and poured the tea, the sound of liquid sloshing into the cups filling the silence.

"Even if you're right, an antidote for belladonna means nothing."

Titus began to protest, but she raised a hand to stop him. "I've worked with it for decades, that and all the other medicinal plants. I know when to use them and when to hold off. You're not telling me anything new. Believe me, I have tried everything. The magic is responsible for mutation. The belladonna might carry it, but magic is the key."

She fell silent and took a sip of her drink.

Titus sighed and shook his head. "I had hoped that somehow this might be new knowledge, that there was a simple way to stop the abomination."

Kabila smiled kindly. "Life is never simple." She put her cup down. "And now I have something for you." The midwife rose and bent to a low cupboard, opened it and pulled a package from within. She handed it to Titus. "This came late last night by messenger from the rebel base."

Kabila put her hand on his arm, squeezing gently, with an expression Titus had seen on her face before when she told families of a death. A deep sense of foreboding rose within him.

He took the package, recognizing the handwriting from one of the women who cared for Maria and other addicts in the rebel camp. He tore open the seal and unwrapped it, barely constraining the sob that rose within at what he saw.

The necklace he had given to Maria on their wedding day, a tiny silver hummingbird representing the grace and speed at which she moved and the pace of their love. A folded note lay alongside it.

Titus flattened it out with one trembling hand as cold fear spread through his limbs. His vision blurred as tears ran down his cheeks, dropping onto the ink. He wanted to wash away the terrible words and then perhaps they could not be true.

"She's dead," he gasped. "She died giving birth to a mis-shapen corpse. A monster."

As he sank to the floor, Finn knelt with him and Titus sobbed into his friend's embrace as he clutched the tiny hummingbird in one fist.

Images of their love flooded back to him — stolen kisses in the library, lazy hours entwined under the apple trees in the orchard, running together over the hills, the sound of Maria's laugh echoing across the valley. He would never touch her skin again, never feel safe in her embrace, never hear her say his name. His heart emptied, each tear wrung from his wretched soul.

After the wave of despair passed over, Titus let the rage come. He would avenge Maria's death. He had nothing left to lose.

He pulled away from Finn and wiped his eyes. "We go east to the camp where they make Liberation. There's a munitions store on the way. We'll get explosives and stop this thing at the source."

Finn nodded. "I'm with you, brother."

CHAPTER 8

Sienna walked out of the medical wing with Rachel's warning echoing through her mind and a vision of the young woman's hand clutching at the sheets, white-knuckled as she faced an unending nightmare. Would she end up that way if she crossed the border once more?

"Sienna, wait a moment."

Her father's voice made her turn and Sienna waited in the corridor for him to catch up.

John Farren's gait was hobbled, his back torn beyond repair from the tortures of the dungeon below the Castle of the Shadow. He kept the suffering from his face most of the time, but Sienna knew that chronic pain tormented him at night, and plagued his waking hours. She had once believed her father lost on an expedition many years ago, and perhaps it was best to think that was still true. She had not told her mother that he still lived, partly because those old wounds had healed and they had both moved on, but also because of Bridget. Sienna had glimpsed the love between her father and the new Illuminated, but there was little hope for them now to act upon those feelings. Sienna could only hope that she and Finn could transcend their different paths and find a way to be together.

As her father reached her, Sienna wrapped her arms

around him, clasping his shoulders, careful not to press against his back. John winced a little, then relaxed into her hug, putting his arms around her in his turn. They stood for a moment, breathing together. Sienna could hear his heartbeat, still strong in his chest, the magic that ran through both their veins part of a long line of Blood Mapwalkers. There were so few of them left now, and still so much to do on both sides of the border.

John pulled away. "Be careful over there." His blue eyes darkened, like waves upon a storm-borne sea. "The balance of power has shifted and there is nothing in the annals to help us navigate this new time."

"It will be okay, Dad. Mila and Perry will be with me, and I'm sure we'll get through, find Finn and the Resistance and work with them."

John shook his head. "A cross-border alliance has never worked. Our worlds are ever more divergent and the Borderlanders are right to want their share of wealth. I fear it is too late for compromise."

Sienna smiled. "Your generation tried one way, now let mine try another. The Ministry has survived much, and it will continue on, I promise."

John bent forward and kissed her forehead. "I'm proud of you," he whispered. "And I know your grandfather would be, too. Go safe."

* * *

A few hours later, Zoe joined the Mapwalker team in the Gallery of Geographical Maps. She looked around with fascination at the long corridor, its walls painted with bird's-eye scenes of distant lands. Each was a portal, a simple way to travel through space and time with minimal use of Mapwalker magic.

They stood in front of a map of modern Egypt, made notable by the disruption of the Nile by Lake Nasser, but Zoe could see traces of another layer beneath, a magical map that would allow them to travel through. Now she had learned to shift her vision, she could not unsee the contours of the world beneath the real. It gave her a mild sense of vertigo even at this level. How much more would she feel if she navigated the threads below? She tried to quash her fear, digging her nails into her palms. She was determined to be worthy of this assignment.

Mila and Perry stood with backpacks on, faces set with determination as they gazed into the desert land before them. Both were around her age, but they had an air of experience that Zoe lacked. Mila moved with a liquid grace, but Zoe had heard tales of her ability to hold her own in a fight. Perry was muscular, his arms bulging against the seams of his jacket, his face that of a young god. He looked over and gave a smile. Zoe blushed a little as their eyes locked. Perhaps this trip wouldn't be so bad, after all.

The door opened, and Sienna walked in with a palpable sense of purpose. She walked to the map of Egypt and then turned to face Zoe.

"Have you traveled this way before?"

Zoe shook her head.

Sienna smiled and held out a hand. "Just hold on and keep breathing."

Mila and Perry gathered round and laid their hands on Sienna's. She reached out with her other hand and entered the map.

Zoe watched the golden threads part and suddenly, they were inside the fabric itself. She tried to catch her breath, but the rush was like a wind tunnel. It was all she could do to keep her balance as nausea rose violently inside. Sounds of rushing water surrounded her, a cacophony that made her want to cover her ears, but she couldn't let go of Sienna for fear of being trapped here between the threads of the world.

Under the sound of the storm, Zoe heard a voice.

Sienna.

A voice made up of thousands of souls, a sound that made her both shiver in fear and want to run toward it. Something seductive and powerful, something that promised the world and only asked one thing in return.

A bump. A crash.

The ground rushed up to meet her and Zoe tumbled to the desert floor, retching and coughing, spitting up the bile that rose in her mouth. Her head throbbed, her muscles ached. If this was mapwalking, then she'd stick with an airplane next time.

Zoe groaned and rolled onto her back. The sky brooded with heavy rain clouds and a falcon hovered in the warm air currents high above; the bird representing Horus, the Egyptian god of the sky and protector of the realm. Its cry pierced the air, a haunting sound of melancholy.

"Here, drink this." Perry handed her a bottle of water. Zoe sat up and took a sip. "First time is rough. But you get used to it."

Mila gave a terse laugh as she dusted herself off. "Well, some people do."

Sienna stood a little way off, looking out over the lip of a quarry. She turned as they reached her and for a moment she caught Zoe's gaze, a question in her eyes. The voice — perhaps the others had never heard it — but now was not the time to speak of what it might mean. Zoe gave a slight nod and a look of understanding passed between them.

"Wow, look at this place." Perry gazed out across the valley, a deep scar in the earth pitted with excavation, as the others came to stand with him.

"The great monuments of ancient Egypt were built from this rock," Zoe said. "The land was barren outside the reaches of the Nile, the only place where human life could thrive, but this place made their construction possible."

Countless slaves toiled and died here, their blood soaking the earth, augmenting the coppery red of the layers below. In the millennia since, the quarry had been partially filled in by the sands of the desert. A ruined village on the southern edge showed evidence that man had tried to flourish here, but rumors of a cursed land and the inhospitable landscape kept people away for generations.

Mila shivered as a sharp wind blew across the desert, sending whirlwinds of sand and dust into the air. Clouds gathered overhead and a roll of thunder sounded in the distance. "We need to get moving. That storm's heading straight for us." She turned to Zoe. "So how do we get in?"

Zoe flushed a little, suddenly the center of attention. "Well, um, I think …" The words were heavy in her mouth and it seemed as if everything she knew dissolved to incoherence now they were in the field. She had only ever dealt with manuscripts and papyri, never the genuine thing. This place was three-dimensional, it had texture, it had weather, and the team looked to her to take control.

After a beat of silence, Sienna pointed down the valley. "It looks like there's a change in the rock strata down there. What do you think?"

Zoe knew Sienna was trying to help and the moment of respite allowed a shift in her perspective. As she looked down the valley, she called to mind the papyrus map back at her desk in the Ministry. It had been too fragile to carry with them, but she had committed every detail to memory. She thought of the golden threads and how she had to see differently to allow them to emerge.

She closed her eyes for a second and then opened them again, focusing not on the landscape but in the surrounding air, softening her gaze until … Zoe gasped, grinning in delight as the world shifted and suddenly she could see the warp and weft of threads that held the environment together. There was a knot of stitches in the valley below and filaments that stretched down into the earth. It must be the opening to the funerary complex.

"What is it? What can you see?"

Sienna's voice startled Zoe, and the threads dissolved as quickly as they had appeared.

"I ... I saw the complex down there. I know the way now."

Zoe stumbled a little, suddenly weak, her head spinning.

Sienna put a hand out to steady her. "Careful now, we don't want to lose you so soon." Her voice was gentle. "Do you know how to use your weaver magic?"

Zoe looked into her eyes, meeting the young woman's more experienced gaze. "I thought it was just for restoration, but I think there might be more to it. I can see threads running through the earth, binding the world."

Sienna smiled. "There are often surprising elements to our gifts. Don't worry. We've all been through it. Just trust that it will emerge at the right time." As she spoke, shadows darkened in her eyes, thunderclouds gathering in a reflection of the storm above. Zoe blinked, and they were gone.

The team set off down the edge of the quarry, slip-sliding on the scree, careful not to trip over the rocks. The wind picked up and funneled through the valley, whistling through piles of strewn boulders like a warning in this desolate place. But there was life even here, clumps of prickly shrubs with small leathery leaves and tiny succulents with sharp spines. Zoe caught sight of a small furry creature darting under a rock as they approached, maybe one of the desert gerbils endemic to the area. As she turned her head to watch it run, she skidded on the loose stones. Perry reached out a hand to steady her.

"Careful, we need you." He smiled and Zoe's heart beat a little faster. Did he hold her hand for just a second longer than was necessary?

Rain pattered down as the Mapwalkers reached the bottom of the valley. By the time they made it to where Zoe thought the entrance would be, it poured down in sheets of wind that slammed against the rocks as if nature itself tried to stop their progress. They were all soaked through, dripping wet, cold and desperate to get under shelter.

They hurried to a pile of enormous blocks of stone, each one carved from the quarry and discarded here — or perhaps placed specifically to camouflage the entrance. Zoe relaxed her gaze and once again, saw the golden thread weaving its way through.

"This is definitely it."

Perry frowned. "How do we get inside? There's no way we can move these blocks ourselves."

Sienna placed her hands on the stone pile. "Now we're here, I can draw a map and take us inside."

Mila shook her head. "No need. But you all need to stand way back if I'm going to do this."

The others walked up and away from the entrance, high enough to be out of range but still close enough to see. Zoe's skin tingled with the cold of the rain but also with the anticipation of what might happen, of the thrill of being here with the Mapwalker team.

As the storm raged above them, Mila lifted her hands, then her face to the rain. Her clothes were soaked through and it was as if her skin underneath became one with the water. Mila reached for the deluge and brought it down in a torrent, using it to sweep under one of the heavy stone blocks and move it to the side of the entrance, lifting and floating it away as if on flood waters. She directed the rain as a symphony, sweeping it down from the heavens above and swirling the rocks away from the entrance. Mila's face rippled with joy as the surge washed around her. This was her element, and Zoe felt a sense of privilege to see the Waterwalker so transformed. Would she ever be that confident in her magic?

Once she had uncovered the entrance, Mila swirled the

water away from the quarry floor, pinning her flood behind the barrier of rocks now placed like a dam to one side. But it didn't stop the rainfall that still poured down upon them, trickling down into the revealed mouth of the complex below.

Mila beckoned, and the team jogged back down to the entrance. "Let's get inside, then I'll seal it up behind us with some rocks. We don't want a flood following us down there."

Zoe stepped inside the rough-hewn tunnel, chisel marks still visible in the stone overhead. It was just big enough for them to walk upright, although Perry's head almost touched the ceiling. As they descended, torches in hand, she wondered about the forgotten people who had dug this place, whether they had died here, their bones becoming part of history.

As they rounded a corner out of sight of the entrance, Mila dropped back and a moment later, a resounding crash echoed through the tunnel. Flakes of rock dropped from the ceiling from thin fissures above that seemed to widen as they watched. Zoe held her breath, aware of the tons of rock above, suddenly conscious that they were now barricaded in an ancient tomb, their only way out now blocked by impenetrable slabs of stone. There was no turning back.

A thin stream of water trickled down the tunnel as Mila rounded the corner once more, her footsteps a little weary as the magic took its toll. But Zoe could see that the tattooed Waterwalker welcomed the price for the joy it gave her in the moment.

As the team came together again, Perry led them on. "Let's see what's down here."

He walked on with confident steps as the tunnel wound down into the earth. Zoe recalled that the chambers of the complex were several stories down, so they were probably entering from one of the side tunnels. Etchings marked the walls of the corridor and occasionally, a few crude paintings, but nothing of the skill or importance of the art in the Valley of the Kings. These were only rudimentary slashes and fragments of curses that Zoe recognized from funerary texts. Nothing remarkable. Could this really be the right place?

They turned a last corner and Perry stopped in surprise; the others halting quickly behind him.

The tunnel ended in a low doorway, a crawl space into blackness beyond. Above it, an ancient god looked down upon them with eyes of deep blue lapis lazuli, its hideous features a dire warning. The head of a Nile river crocodile, jagged teeth dripping with blood, its forelegs the powerful body of a lion and its rear, the thick hide of a hippopotamus. It was carved into the rock and outlined in precious stones, surrounded by curses etched deep into stone.

"Ammit, devourer of the dead," Zoe whispered. "Made up of the three dread creatures the Egyptians feared the most. He eats the hearts of the impure if they are weighed and found wanting."

Mila bent down and shone her torch into the black hole. "And we're meant to crawl into this?" She looked up at Zoe. "Are you sure this is the right way?"

Sienna stepped forward. "It's the Map of the Impossible, it's not going to be a walk in the park, is it?" She pointed up to a series of hieroglyphics. "I recognize these from my grandfather's journal. This has to be the right way."

She bent down and crawled into the dark, the light from her torch vanishing quickly. Zoe held her breath, part of her expecting to hear a scream, a crash, a moan.

A moment later, Sienna's excited voice came echoing back. "You guys need to come and see this."

CHAPTER 9

IT WAS A RELIEF to get away from the image of the devouring god and out of the constricting tunnel. The vault stretched away into the shadows, the far end out of sight, but the echo of their voices showed how large the space was. Perry stood up, looking around as Mila and Zoe brushed dust from their clothes. His gaze lingered on the restorer for a moment. Something about her made him want to know more. Perhaps this mission would give him the opportunity.

Sienna stood shining her torchlight ahead. "What is this place?"

Her words were clearly directed at Zoe, the only one of them who knew much about ancient Egypt, but Perry couldn't help but feel it was a broader question. They had thought this was some kind of entrance to the Borderlands, perhaps a simple portal like the gate in the Circus at Bath, but this was far more than a doorway.

It was some kind of antechamber and bundles of cloth covered every inch of the floor, discolored with age, dirty yellow-brown wrappings around a bulbous center.

"What are they?" Perry nudged one with his toe, grimacing as it rolled heavily to the side, crunching on a layer of loose stones beneath. "Ugh. There's definitely something in there."

He shivered a little, trying not to imagine what lay inside.

Zoe bent to look at the bundle more closely. "The Egyptians mummified all kinds of creatures. Cats, crocodiles, mice and ibis amongst them."

Mila shone her torch at the wall, illuminating paintings of hundreds of birds. Hooked bills like scythes, black eyes made of obsidian beads that flashed as the light touched them, as if they watched the intruders from centuries past.

"I guess they're ibis, but why so many?"

Zoe pulled out a pen from her pack and used the end to prod at the mummified creature, trying to ease the wrappings aside. "There might be amulets here, evidence of what they represent. I've read of sacrificial chambers at Sakkara with thousands of dead ibis inside, offerings to Thoth—"

"God of wisdom, writing and magic," Sienna finished for her.

Zoe looked up. "Yes, you know of him?"

"My grandfather's journal contains much about Thoth, postulating that the priests who served him were some of the earliest Mapwalkers. Those who combined writing and magic, who created living worlds with their inscriptions — and their paintings."

"Makes sense," Perry said as he took a tentative step forward, trying not to tread on any of the shrouded bodies. "But whatever the reason, we have to get through this chamber. Let's move on."

He took another step, holding out his arms for balance as he gingerly tiptoed around the ancient corpses. The thought of the dust and bones and feathers and dried blood of millennia made him want to get out of there fast. The others gathered their things and followed in his footsteps.

A crunch as Perry stepped on more of the loose stones. These were larger chunks, and he rolled a little on his ankle. Steadying himself, he looked down, the light from his headtorch reflecting off ... what was that? He bent down to look more closely and then stood up sharply. The others stopped at his alarm.

"Bones. Human, by the look of them." He pointed down, not wanting to move for the unbearable crunch that would inevitably come.

Sienna crouched down and examined the detritus on the chamber floor. "You're right. Human bones, dismembered. They have weird patterns on them, like tiny slashes. I wonder …" She looked up at the wall paintings where the ibis stood on the banks of the Nile, their beaks like scythes.

As she spoke, Perry saw a movement in the darkness near the wall, as if a shudder passed through one of the bundles. Mila saw it too and shone her light toward it, just as the mummies began to twitch and shake. Perry frowned, a moment of confusion before he realized what was happening.

The things inside were trying to get out.

"Move!" Mila shouted as the shuddering spread across the floor, the bundles rolling and lurching. The thud of bodies hitting each other and bumping against the walls echoed about the chamber as clouds of dust rose into the air.

The Mapwalkers ran through the field of mummified creatures, covering their mouths as they coughed, eyes streaming as dust obscured the way.

Perry led them on, no longer caring where his feet landed, relishing the crunch of bodies under his stride, each one a broken beast that could no longer emerge from the grave.

A cry behind him.

Perry stopped and spun round.

Zoe had slipped and fallen amongst the mummies. As he bent to help her up, he felt the sudden weight of bodies on his back, the slash of tiny knives on his skin. He jerked up and shook himself, seeing for the first time the horror that emerged from the dusty haze.

The remains of mummified ibis, dried flesh hanging from their skeletons, eyes coal black holes in elongated skulls and beaks like sickles, slashing back and forth. They shrieked together, high-pitched calls over guttural grunts, the volume growing as more escaped the bonds of their ancient wrapping.

Two more leapt for him.

Perry pushed Zoe behind his back, shielding her as he opened his palm and released his fire magic. The remains of the two creatures fell to the bone-covered floor. Almost immediately, the burned parts twitched and began to re-form into a semblance of a creature, parts of one subsumed into the other — a hybrid corpse.

Perry shuddered as he directed his flame down and finished it off, leaving only ash this time.

Sienna and Mila fought the creatures alongside, batting them away with torches and kicking the birds as they attacked from below. Zoe regained her balance and swung her pack like a mace, using it to beat the birds off.

Together, they could keep the ibis at bay for now … but they kept coming.

There were so many in the chamber, waves of shrieking dead birds with thousands more to be born anew from the bundles of wrapping that shuddered as the Mapwalkers progressed through the cave. They had to get out of here.

"Follow me!" Perry stepped past Zoe and sent his flame into the darkness ahead, burning a path through the writhing bundles, turning them to ash before they could even emerge. He turned and hurled balls of flame either side of Sienna and Mila, freeing them enough so they could follow.

Together, the four Mapwalkers darted through the tomb, beating back any birds that made it through, pursued by inhuman shrieks.

The end of the chamber emerged through smoke and dust. A solid wall painted with images of ibis slaughtering worshippers of Thoth, bloody limbs hacked from torsos, heads rolling as the birds overran the temple grounds. An avian massacre dedicated to the god who ruled them.

"How do we get out of here?" Sienna shouted above the din of screeches, pounding on the wall with her fists.

"There must be a way." Zoe scanned the wall for anything that might help. "The priests of Thoth would have made a door. The god is often shown carrying an *ankh* symbol, the key to life. Look for that."

Perry stepped in front of them, forming a barricade of fire to keep the birds away as the others scoured the wall, searching for a way out. He could feel the slow creep of shadow seeping into his veins as he blasted the enlivened carcasses, the stink of burned feathers and desiccated flesh filling his senses. This place drained more of him than it should. Something in the atmosphere seemed to deaden his very life force. They had not considered what might rule this place between the worlds, or the risk in crossing it. But it was too late to turn back.

"Hurry, I can't keep this up for too much longer."

Perry understood the price of his magic, and he accepted the risk, even knowing what his father had become. Sir Douglas was one of the great Shadow Cartographers, but Perry was still haunted by the image Sienna had painted of him on their return from the refugee camp on the last mission. She said he was closer to shadow than man now, his material self more inconsequential every day. Perry only wished to reach his father before the end — and have enough flame to finish the man himself.

A skittering noise broke through the roar of the inferno.

The clatter of skeletal feet.

The ibis surged over the barrier of flame, running up the walls and across the ceiling in some perversion of gravity, scything their beaks back and forth as they dive-bombed Perry.

He swung one hand above, burning them with a lance of fire as they dropped. A stinking rain of ash fell in their wake.

Perry retched as it filled his mouth and nose and eyes, chunks of stinking cadaver collecting around his feet. As the birds continued to advance in an unrelenting wave, Perry knew they would drown here in the dust of the dead in this god-forsaken place.

CHAPTER 10

"Here!" Zoe shouted.

The clunk of levers and the sound of stone rasping over sand.

Perry surged his flame into the birds in a final blast of magic. As hands pulled him back into a dark cavity, he burned the last of the ibis, pushing them away as the door swung shut. He sank to the ground, retching and gagging as he spat out the remains of the dead creatures, the taste of the grave lingering in his mouth.

Perry explosively coughed up the last of the feathers, then sank back against the cool stone. "I really don't want to go through that again."

Sienna reached out and placed a finger on his lips, her eyes flashing a warning as she pointed into the chamber beyond.

They sat on a wide ledge above a gigantic cave, the cold of the rock and freezing air a welcome relief from the claustrophobic heat of the ibis chamber.

Mila shone her torchlight out over the expanse, illuminating a roiling, churning mass of serpents below, like an undulating sea. They were all different sizes and colors, writhing together, hissing and rattling at the disturbance above. The giant loop of a colossal snake rose from the mass, each black scale as tall as a man, the powerful musculature of its body pulsing as it moved, slithering beneath its kin. An ancient creature, formed from magic and nightmares.

"Apep," Zoe whispered, her eyes wide. "The giant serpent, embodiment of chaos, sworn enemy of light and truth, devourer of souls."

Perry slumped back against the wall and sighed. "Seriously?"

Sienna pulled her grandfather's journal from her pack and opened it to the pages of hieroglyphics and sketches of the underworld path.

"Here." She pointed to the hand-drawn map. "After the guardians of the gate, presumably the ibis, there is a path of snake charmers. A way through the chamber of serpents."

Zoe pointed at the page. "This also says there is a high path, past the watchers. Perhaps that could be the better way?"

Mila turned her torch toward the ceiling of the chamber. Stalactites dripped from the roof of the cave, some sharp as a blade, others bulbous and curved. They glistened in the light as crystals within flashed with colors of turquoise and emerald, opal and gold. Droplets of water ran down to splash on the serpents below.

Then the light caught what lay beyond and between the needles of rock. Leathery cocoons, over six feet in length, each hanging down over the space below. Each pulsing with life.

"The watchers," Zoe whispered.

Mila thought of the winged statues she had seen in front of the sunken pyramid beneath Ganvié, a battalion of dark angels ready to fight. Could these cocoons be their resting place? She had wished to see such miraculous creatures in the flesh, but down here in the realm of the dead, that suddenly seemed like a bad idea.

Sienna shone her torchlight below the cocoons, following

a scar in the wall, a narrow path between the serpents below and the unknown creatures above. "That way," she said. "As quietly and as carefully as possible."

* * *

Zoe saw the sense in Sienna's choice, but it didn't make it any less terrifying. The ledge curved around out of sight to the left of the cave, a precarious track, wet with dripping water. It looked slippery with only the rock to grasp onto and a precipitous drop to the pit of serpents below.

Perry's magic could be useful if they needed to fight, but he looked exhausted, drained from the battle with the ibis. He struggled to stand, pulling himself up from the wall as they prepared to leave the safety of the ledge. Zoe wanted to reach out and help him up, but she turned away. Perhaps he didn't want to be seen in a moment of weakness.

Mila had also used her magic recently, opening the tomb and controlling the flood, while Sienna had mapwalked them all here from the Ministry. Each of them weakened, drops of shadow pooling in their blood, while her own magic was but a faint glimmer, an almost useless gift.

For a moment, Zoe wished she were back in the calm, safe world of Antiquities, the smell of old books, ink and coffee with the occasional sound of a turning page. No reanimated corpses to fight, no ancient Egyptian nightmares to run from — but no miracles either, no friends with magic in their fingertips, no sense of wonder.

"Are you coming?" Sienna asked softly, as she stood at the edge of the way ahead.

Zoe nodded. "I'll follow you."

The Mapwalker team crept in single file along the trail, Sienna in the lead, then Zoe, with Perry and Mila behind. Zoe hugged the rock face, edging almost sideways to keep as much of her body weight away from the precipice as possible. They walked on in silence, their breath frosting in the air.

Suddenly, Sienna tripped on a rock.

She clutched at the wall and righted herself, but tiny stones skittered off the path, disappearing into the writhing serpents beneath.

Zoe held her breath as the giant snake paused in its movement at the sound. Its head was still buried under the sea of squirming creatures and she really didn't want to see what happened if it emerged.

She had read of Apep's battle with the sun god, Ra, his magical gaze freezing the deity, his undulating body creating earthquakes in the world above. His terrifying roar was said to cause the underworld to shake as he devoured those who trespassed in his realm. To banish chaos and evil, the priests of ancient Egypt would build an effigy of the serpent every year and burn it for protection against the darkness — but the snake would rise again once more.

After a beat of silence, they inched along the track, each halting footstep placed carefully to stay quiet, hands reaching for holes in the rock wall to help steady the way. Sienna turned a corner where the path narrowed even more, disappearing out of sight. Zoe reached a hand around the edge to balance herself—

Her fingers brushed against something hairy, something with thick legs. She gasped as a sharp pain pierced the back of her hand. She jerked her arm back from the rock, glimpsing the orbed body of a spider squatting in the hole as she took a step back — into nothing, falling, tumbling away from the path.

Perry reached for her, his fingers brushing hers, but he couldn't get a grip.

Zoe screamed, her cry echoing around the chamber.

Time slowed, her vision narrowing as she fell, the eyes of the Mapwalkers upon her, helpless to stop her descent.

In that moment of terror, Zoe shifted her vision, and the cave was at once patterned with strings of light and cords of shadow, both making up the weave of the underworld.

Zoe reached for the strands, spinning them into a net of star and shade with the liquidity of water and the strength of rock. It cushioned her fall and held her above the sea of serpents on a web of gold. She lay there, stunned, hardly able to believe what she had just done.

The hiss of the creatures below intensified at the disruption.

"Move!" Mila shouted down.

Perry and Sienna pointed in desperation at something behind her. "Get up here!"

Zoe turned on the web, leaning on its bonds, comfortable in its embrace, sure of her safety — to see the giant serpent rearing up from below.

Its head was flint grey with sharp angular scales, its mouth open as it lunged with bared fangs. Zoe rolled sideways across the weft of strands, the snake's head passing by her so closely that she could feel the rush of air and smell the sulfur stink of its breath.

A drop of its venom fell onto the web, dissolving the cords. The lattice collapsed beneath her.

Zoe clambered away, pulling herself up even as the snake turned to attack once more. Her breath came fast, her arms aching as she tried to haul her body weight up. The golden strings glimmered, flickering in and out as her vision narrowed, her magic fading as fear rose within. She scrambled faster, looking up to the Mapwalkers above. She had to get to them.

Mila stood on the edge of the path, her arms outstretched. She drew drops of water to her from the dripping rocks, spinning them into what looked like a whip.

As the snake lunged for Zoe, Mila lashed out, smashing the creature's head with a spear of icy water. It stopped and turned at the sting, giving Zoe a little more time to pull herself closer to the rock. She climbed, only meters from safety now.

"Come on!" Sienna called down.

Perry lay on the path and reached for her. "Just a few more meters. You can do it!"

Zoe could see the desperation in his eyes, the hope of safety in his outstretched hand.

The snake hissed and lunged again. Mila cracked the whip once more, but the serpent ignored the barb this time, charging at Zoe's dangling legs as she hung from the rock, exhausted and panting with fear. As she looked back, it was as if the Shadow came to life in the creature, knitted together from darkness and magic, its only purpose to protect the way between the worlds.

It opened its mouth wider, closer now. Zoe felt pinned by its stare, hypnotized by the black gleam of obsidian—

A crack of pain on her arm, a sting of water. Mila's lasso.

"Grab it!" Zoe snapped out of her reverie and wrapped the water noose around her, using the last of her magic to wrap golden strands around it, turning the liquid into golden threads strong enough to hold.

The Mapwalker team yanked her up and away as the serpent smashed into the wall where Zoe had been just seconds before. Its frustrated hiss filled the cavern, its writhing brethren joining the chorus in a cacophony of reptilian rage.

They lay panting on the narrow ledge. Zoe sat up, her body shaking with the aftermath of the encounter, her clothes wet from the lasso. She looked at Mila.

"Thank you."

Mila shook her head. "You did most of it. What happened down there anyway? We saw you suspended in thin air, and you did something to my water lasso to make it hold your weight."

Zoe frowned. "You mean you couldn't see the web?"

They all shook their heads. Sienna looked at Zoe with interest. "Your weaver magic seems to be far more than just mending maps."

Perry touched Zoe's arm. "Are you okay?" She looked up into his blue eyes and noted the genuine concern.

"I'm just a little shaky. I'll be okay."

Perry helped her up, his strong arms a welcome sanctuary. "We should get moving—"

A screech cut through the cavern, an inhuman sound like nails scratching on flint, like ice shearing off the face of a berg. Then the flap of giant wings in the dark.

CHAPTER 11

A GIANT BAT FLEW across the cavern toward the Mapwalker team. Its leathery wings were several meters across with ragged claws halfway along. Thick black fur covered its body but its face was hairless, pale skin, an abomination of ridges and scars, an upturned snout above a mouth of razor-sharp teeth. As it dived for the team, it raised its hind legs, each toe topped with a sharp blade to slash its prey to pieces.

The Mapwalkers pressed themselves against the rock, making as small a target as possible. The bat's claws scraped against the stone above, sending a shower of sparks down upon them.

As it flew past and wheeled up into the air, Sienna pushed off from the wall. "Run!"

A ripping sound echoed through the chamber, like flesh torn by a ravenous predator. The cocoons split apart and more giant bats emerged from their sleep, dropping into the black, screeching as they flocked together in a dark mass.

The sound of their cries thrummed through Zoe's body, the pulse of the underworld creating a rhythm along with their running feet. They darted along the path, each footstep on the edge of the precipice, but Zoe was no longer afraid of falling. Something had shifted when she fell, her confidence rising as she learned more about her magic.

The bats dived for them in waves, swiping with sharp claws as the Mapwalker team crouched and ducked and hid in crevices as they ran on. One creature caught Perry's pack, lifting him from the ground. He reached back and shot a ball of flame into the bat. It dropped him quickly, its cry of pain sending the others into a frenzy.

But Zoe could see the toll even this little bit of magic took on Perry. He was still exhausted from the battle with the ibis and they all needed to rest — but there was no respite from the attack.

Sienna ran on, shouting and waving her arms to attract the creatures. "Over here!"

They dive-bombed her, leaving the others alone for a moment, enough time for Perry to catch his breath. Zoe turned back to see Sienna crouching under an overhang, several of the bats scraping at it, trying to pull her out with long talons.

"How much further?" Mila asked in frustration. "This cave is never ending. It's like we're running in circles."

Her words echoed in Zoe's mind, reminding her of something she had seen in the three-dimensional map back in the Ministry, a cavern spiraling into darkness.

"You're right." She pointed down into the mass of snakes below. "It's a circle. The way out is through the bottom of the chamber."

Mila shook her head. "Might have been useful information a little earlier."

Zoe flushed. "I'm sorry, I—"

"A little help over here, guys!" Sienna shouted from beneath the overhang.

Mila spun her water whip, pulling down droplets from the stalactites. She lashed out at the bats, harder now, with a vortex of spinning liquid interspersed with particles of rock. She ripped into the wings of the bats, dark blood spurting from them as they screamed and wheeled away. But above them, the next wave of creatures prepared to dive.

Sienna ran back to where the others stood, her face red with effort, panting for breath. "What are you waiting for? We have to go on."

Mila pointed down. "Apparently it's that way."

Zoe nodded. "I'm so sorry. I only just remembered that the map had a chamber like the circles of hell. The way out is through the bottom."

Perry pointed ahead in the gloom. "She's right. Look, that's where we came in. We've almost run a circle of this damned place."

They gazed down into the mass of serpents, the giant one undulating at the center like an angry god.

"But how do we get down there?" Sienna wondered aloud.

"We jump," Zoe said, a plan forming in her mind even as she shifted her gaze in the cavern. Strings of light and shadow emerged from the darkness, forming a pattern that overlaid the creatures of nightmare. A well of power rose within and she reached out, fingers entwining strands in the air, creating a funnel down into the depths.

"You know we can't see anything, right?" Perry said, his voice doubtful. "You expect us to jump into nothing. Toward them." He pointed down at the pit of snakes.

"You have your magic, I have mine," Zoe said.

Sienna nodded. "We're a team. We trust each other."

Her words gave Zoe a flush of pride, a recognition that she was truly a Mapwalker. But there was no time to enjoy the feeling now. They still had to get out of here alive.

She wove the threads together and then opened them up, creating a space between the serpents below, a funnel of light patterned with shadow. Both needed to make up the underworld.

As she manipulated the strings, Zoe felt eyes upon her. Not the eyes of the team, but something behind the creatures that surrounded them. Something gazed through the deformed snakes and bats, a knowing presence. Zoe shuddered as she felt its icy chill and worked faster. They had to get out of here.

"It's done."

Mila looked into the darkness. "I still don't see anything."

"You won't, but it's there. A funnel of strings that will take us down to the exit below."

"Will it hold if those creatures attack?" Sienna asked.

Zoe shrugged. "I hope so." A screech from above. "But let's not wait around to find out." She looked at the team. "You trust Sienna to walk you through the map. Trust me now."

She stepped out into blackness, shimmering strands of the weave world around her. A sense of power thrummed in the cords as she slid down the funnel toward the rock wall below. The net shifted with the weight of the others as they followed Zoe down. She rested her hands on the strings, sending energy back up to them, cushioning her friends, surrounding them with light. The gleam reflected off the scales of the serpents as they pushed against the lattice, but Zoe knew they could not penetrate her magic — as long as she could hold it together.

She reached the bottom of the cave floor and stood, arms raised, as the others landed around her. Behind them, a round boulder blocked the way ahead.

Mila rolled up to stand. "That was pretty crazy."

"I can't hold the lattice for much longer." Zoe felt the push of the serpents increase behind the light, the weight of their bodies, their slithering presence and hissing sound permeating her net.

One tiny snake dropped through. Perry stamped on its head, crushing it to a pulp. "Then let's get out of here. Help me with this."

Together they pushed the boulder away from the tunnel mouth and eased inside. It was big enough for two abreast if they crouched away from the low ceiling. Mila and Sienna went in first, and Perry helped Zoe inside. She backed away, pulling her net closer and closer, until finally, she used it to pull the boulder back in front of them.

In the darkness beyond, thick bodies thudded against stone as the snakes tried to reach them. But the barrier held.

Perry opened his palm, holding a flicker of light aloft as the four of them cowered in the tunnel. Zoe saw her own exhaustion reflected in the faces of the others. They were physically drained and almost spent of magic. They couldn't fight another battle today.

Mila pulled Kendal Mint Cake from her pack, broke off some pieces and they ate in silence, letting the sugar sweetness return some energy.

"Where next?" Perry asked. "What's at the end of this tunnel? Please, not another creature cavern."

"From what I can remember, it's not much further," Zoe said softly. "We've almost made it through." Her words sounded convincing, but she still felt a presence in the caves, something watching them, something aware of their trespass.

Sienna nodded. "We need to get out of this cave system before we rest. Come on." She got up and walked on, half-crouched, along the tunnel. Mila slowly followed, stretching her limbs as if frozen from the chill of the cave.

Perry helped Zoe up. "That was impressive," he whispered. "Nicely done."

Zoe flushed, appreciating his words as she walked ahead of him in the tunnel, his tiny light a welcome warmth at her back.

* * *

Sienna kept her face toward the tunnel ahead, even as Perry's flame lit the way from behind. She didn't want the others to see her expression because she was terrible at hiding her thoughts and right now, they were dark indeed.

A Shadow presence watched them, she was sure of it, and she thought Zoe felt it, too. The Weaver was a wildcard and something in her magic called to Sienna's own, like the young woman was always meant to be part of the Mapwalker team. And yet, she seemed to know so little about her gift. Sienna smiled to herself in the darkness. She had been in that position herself not so long ago. Perhaps she was still testing the bounds of her own magic.

Their footsteps echoed in the passage as it looped around, each turn making it harder to sense where they were under the earth. Sienna shivered as the chill air touched her skin, turning her breath to frosted mist as she walked. She could smell minerals in the surrounding rock, metallic with a hint of moss and lichen. It was strange to feel so untethered, to have no place of physical reference. This place negated her own magic, because she needed to know where she was and where she was going in the world. Neither was clear right now.

"What's that?"

Mila's voice brought Sienna back to the rocky tunnel. There was a light ahead, brighter than the reach of Perry's flame. It glowed a warm orange, a welcoming glimmer in the dark and cold of this never-ending cave system. But the biting cold snaked into Sienna's blood as she sensed the Shadow strengthening with every step. This place was no sanctuary, but there was no choice. They had to keep moving onward.

Finally, she clambered out of the end of the tunnel, emerging into a hollowed cavern that stretched high above into darkness. Stone walls with arched doorways created a circular space and above them, hundreds, maybe thousands, of niches cut into the rock, like a mausoleum waiting for the remains of the dead.

The light came from an altar, an enormous slab of rock surrounded by thick beeswax candles. Clearly someone tended the place, but Sienna didn't want to find out who would venture down so far.

Mila walked over to a niche and picked up a sharp-edged rock.

Perry came closer to examine it with her. "Obsidian. Volcanic glass." He looked around at the other niches. "There are many different kinds of rock here. What is this place?"

"The map indicated a temple at the heart of the border," Zoe said. "A place between the worlds."

Sienna sensed a shift in the air, like a breeze from above or the last sigh of a dying soul. Perhaps there had been balance here once upon a time, but now it reeked of decay, withering every second their worlds were held apart.

Mila dropped the obsidian, her hold weakened by the toll of the journey. A crash of rock splintering.

"Sorry! I'm so tired." She shook her head and Perry bent to help as she tried to sweep up the fragments from the ground.

"Ow!" Mila jerked upright as a shard bit into her skin. She held up a finger, a drop of blood rolling down … dripping …

Sienna watched it fall toward the slivers of broken obsidian as it reflected the light like glass. A moment of dread rippled through her as blood touched stone.

A smoky haze rose up.

Mila and Perry stepped back as shadow billowed from the rock, a bloom of darkness that coalesced into the faint shape of a woman. With soft curves draped in folds of silk, her lips a perfect bow, her cheekbones high and aristocratic, she looked like an angel trapped in smoke. She spun around in the mausoleum; her face twisted in grief and madness.

Her eyes darted around the cave — a trapped, tormented soul, desperate for escape.

Her gaze alighted on Sienna, and her expression changed. She bared her teeth, growling like a wild animal, her delicate features dissolving into decaying flesh hanging off a skeletal frame. Her visage shifted to that of a demon as she opened a vast mouth with bloody chunks of flesh inside.

She rushed at Sienna with a howl of rage.

CHAPTER 12

Finn and Titus waited until night fell once more before leaving the safety of the underground hideout for the streets of the trader town. The sounds of raucous laughter came from the usually busy slave square, drunken merchants idling away the hours until their trade in human flesh began once more. While the flow of immigrants had died down when the border closed, they still sold slaves from Uncharted villages to work in the far reaches of the Borderlands. There was no end to the appetite for servants and with the breeding program ever expanding, girls were particularly sought after.

Finn pulled his cloak tighter and ducked into the alleyway behind the houses, heading away in the opposite direction, Titus right behind. They had no time for a fight, but Finn couldn't help but clench his fists in anticipation of such a confrontation. He knew that Titus would appreciate letting out some of his pent-up anger and there could be no more deserving group of self-serving bastards than the slave traders. But they could not attract the attention of the Shadow Guards tonight. They had to get out of town undetected.

They slipped one more time through the warren of streets, ducking and diving into the shelter of shacks, behind shadows cast by ruined walls, a broken place that somehow sustained a pulse of life. Titus took the lead as they emerged from the northern edge, heading away from the desert toward the mountain pass that would lead to the Resistance camp. But instead of heading up to the ridge, they turned into a line of thick forest.

Once they were out of sight of the road, Titus paused, his face turned toward the mountain pass. The air smelled of fresh pine after rain. The hoot of an owl came through the boughs of the trees above, and Finn looked up to see the silhouette of the hunter on the wing.

He waited in silence, watching emotion play over his friend's face as Titus fought the urge to return to the side of his beloved. He imagined Maria up there, her bloody corpse washed and laid beside what was left of the baby. Perhaps they had already been buried.

If Titus wanted to go and mourn them, Finn knew he would proceed alone. He thought of Sienna and wondered if he would ever have a chance to love as Titus did. Such love came at a price, but it was worth trying for. After he had left her in the plague camp that night, Finn's anger had been all-consuming. Sienna had saved her world at the expense of his, but would he have chosen any differently? In the end, we all choose our own tribe over others.

Besides, it was not for the Earthside Mapwalkers to save his people — Borderlanders must save their own. He and Titus were but two of the growing Resistance, but their mission would light a flame that others could follow. The future of the Borderlands did not have to rest with those of the Shadow anymore.

Titus turned, the tracks of tears down his cheeks shining in the moonlight. He took a deep breath and nodded once. "We go on, brother. I will write her name in the sky with the blue flames of the burning crop and honor her death with the end of that which killed her."

He reached out a hand, and they clasped arms, a bond

that went far beyond blood. Finn knew they would rather die together on the mission than return to this place without achieving their goal.

Titus walked on, Finn right behind, as they wove between the trees, their footsteps crunching on a bed of fallen pine needles. The sounds of night hunters came through the branches, the bark of a fox, the roar of a mountain lion in the distance.

When they reached a break in the trees, Titus checked the stars before leading the way once more. Finn hadn't served in this part of the Borderlands. He could navigate around Old Aleppo and its surrounding region with his eyes closed, but here in the mountains, Titus was the expert. He had been with a ranger troop, searching far and wide for resources that the Shadow Cartographers could use in their never-ending war.

As they went on, walking became more like a meditation, their footsteps in time as they marched under shelter of the forest until the fingers of dawn crept across the sky catching the snowcap of the mountain peak high above them.

* * *

As the demon enveloped her, Sienna reached for her magic in a desperate attempt to get away from its grip. But before she could travel, a suffocating mist descended, choking her, wrapping her limbs in a cold dense fog, pinning her arms to her sides. She could hear the cries of the others as they tried to find her, but she was somewhere else now, somewhere between the worlds.

The woman had disappeared, but Sienna could feel her imprint all around. A desperate melancholy. She had lost her child, her family, her home — and her soul. A deep sense of rage throbbed through the air, an anger that would rip flesh from bone to defend a loved one. At the same time, a hopelessness, a desire for oblivion, a need to extinguish life in order to end pain. Sienna doubled over as a wave of anguish washed over her. She cried out in understanding as the world went black.

* * *

"Sienna, Sienna, wake up, please."

The voice was insistent, but Sienna couldn't move. Cold deadened her limbs, heavy with ice, as hard as the obsidian in the surrounding walls, souls trapped within each one.

She opened her eyes. Mila bent over, relief on her face, Perry and Zoe behind, standing close together as if finding solace in one another.

"We couldn't get to you," Mila said. "We thought you were gone."

"It's okay. I know what this place is now," Sienna whispered, her voice croaking from the effort.

Mila helped her sit up, leaning back against the rock wall as Perry passed over a water bottle.

Sienna took several sips before speaking. "This place sits right under the border, at the place where the worlds meet. Sometimes people are lost between Earthside and the Borderlands — over water, in the air, sometimes when the border shifts by deliberate action or chance. These souls are trapped here in obsidian, locked into volcanic rock, creatures of neither world."

Mila looked around at the many thousands of niches, each with a captured soul inside. "Should we smash all the rocks? Set them free?"

Sienna shook her head. "No. They can't exist anymore. They are like flies in amber, captured at the moment of crossing. The woman you released is one with the Shadow now. I don't know if that's any better than where she was."

Sienna couldn't share what else she had experienced — kinship, an affinity within her blood for those between one world and the next. A sense that fate swirled ever closer.

"I'm okay, honestly." She stood up. "The good news is that this is the center of the border, so we're almost on the other side."

Zoe nodded. "Yes, it's not much further." She turned around, her arm outstretched as she pointed at the many arches surrounding them. "We just have to find the right way out."

Sienna found her gaze drawn to the altar. "Can you guys start looking? I need a minute to pull myself together."

Perry and Zoe went in one direction and Mila in the other, working their way around the base of the mausoleum, checking each door for any distinguishing features or a hint of the way forward.

Sienna walked to the altar, the smell of beeswax lingering in the air as the flicker of flame drew her in. The candles were as thick as the waist of a man with multiple wicks designed to burn for months on end. A constant light in the darkness. A representation of hope in every culture.

There was a mosaic above the altar, each tile a precious stone fixed to the rock behind. Its backdrop depicted a vortex of light and shadow, strings of silver and black twisting together in an everlasting web. A representation of balance, perhaps?

Sienna leaned over the altar to examine the mosaic more closely. There were more colors entwined within — a line of rubies scattered amongst the black and silver, behind and between the lines. In the foreground, a young woman clothed in robes of Marian blue stood with upturned palms in surrender, her face lifted to the heavens, her features obscured by silver mist. Scarlet gems streamed from slashes on her arms and with a start, Sienna realized what it showed.

Blood magic at the very heart of the border.

She stepped back, heart pounding, her gaze fixed on the woman whose blood maintained the border. She thought of Bridget back in the Ministry, maps entwined in her veins, ink mingled with her blood. The book on her desk with the sketch of the figure in a vortex of shadow. Could Bridget be the balance?

Or could the voice that called to her from the Tower of the Winds be such a creature? And if so, did that mean its power could never be vanquished?

"Come and look at this." Zoe's voice echoed through the vault. "I think it must be the way out."

Sienna took one last look at the mosaic figure, fixing the image in her mind, then turned away from the altar, pushing down her unease as she joined the others.

The door was thick oak, patterned with intricate carvings of a spiked mountain range. A massive keyhole, far bigger than any human lock, sat under a handle carved in the shape of a lemur.

"Each portal has a distinct image," Zoe explained. "But the map I saw suggested a forest of barbed stone like this image."

Perry shrugged. "It's as good a guess as any and I'm keen to get out of here as fast as possible." He pushed down on the handle. The door didn't budge. He pushed harder, slamming his body against the door, then raised his hands, conjuring his fire, ready to burn their way out.

Zoe placed a hand on his arm. "Wait. Let me try."

She walked to the door and lifted her hands, her fingers weaving in the air in front of the lock. Sienna watched her magic in action, wondering at how Zoe manipulated reality. The weaver magic was most akin to her own, shaping the world anew, gently encouraging a shift that others could only achieve with brute force.

The lock clicked.

Zoe pushed down on the handle, and the door opened.

Sienna smelled the tropical rainforest before she saw it, a heady scent of wet leaves and night flowers that swept into the dead cavern on a warm breeze. It was dark up ahead and as the team walked through the door and into the trees, a bright moon shone above in a field of stars.

The rhythmic chirp of cicadas greeted them as the call of a night bird rang out above and the hoop-hoop of a monkey echoed through the trees. The air was humid and Sienna could feel sweat pooling at the base of her spine as they stood in silence. Was this even the right way?

Between the trees, spiked shards of needle-shaped peaks surrounded them, moonlight reflecting off blades of rock. A narrow path wound through the forest, the way ahead marked by a cairn of stones left by previous travelers.

Mila turned with a smile on her face. "This is the Borderlands. I can feel it."

Sienna nodded. "I sense it, too, but we need to rest before we travel on." The exhaustion of the cave journey crept through her bones, fatigue from physical exertion and the use of magic draining the energy from her. The others must feel the same. She still had a faint unease, but the sense of being watched had dissipated a little. The sounds of the surrounding forest were curiously welcoming, as if they were all just animals seeking shelter for the night.

Perry pointed at a patch of soft ground beneath the canopy of trees with boulders for shelter and support. "This seems good enough." He sank to the forest floor, rolling onto his back, eyes beginning to close already. "Who's taking first watch?"

"I can," Zoe said. "I'm not sleepy right now."

Sienna didn't argue. Now they were out of the cave system, a wave of exhaustion broke over her. Her legs trembled with the aftermath of the soul's connection, her head aching from the intensity of the cavern adventure. Mila looked just as weary as she curled up beside Perry, tugging her coat around her shoulders.

Sienna turned to Zoe. "Wake me in a few hours. I'll take over from you."

Zoe nodded and clambered up onto one of the boulders. She sat cross-legged on the rock and looked up toward the stars shining brightly above. A moonbeam touched the young woman's hair with a silver sheen and Sienna caught the peaceful smile that spread across her face.

She turned away and lay down next to Mila, pulling her pack under her head as a pillow. A tendril of fear snaked into her mind as she closed her eyes. Would there be demons in her nightmares, creatures of smoke and claw? But this time, the wave of fatigue swept her into oblivion.

* * *

Zoe relished the time alone, her mind still circling around the events in the caves. She had entered the chambers as an outsider but she had emerged with a sense of connection with the Mapwalker team, a knowledge that her magic was just as useful as theirs — and dare she think it? Perhaps even more so.

She looked down at her sleeping friends; her gaze lingering on Perry. His fingers twitched as if he dreamed of wielding his magic, and Zoe remembered how he had looked in the cave of the ibis. His hands raised within a tower of flame, his muscular frame silhouetted against the blaze, every inch like a young god of fire. They were so different and yet, there was a connection between them.

Zoe smiled as she leaned back against the cool of the rock and looked up at the stars, shifting her gaze to let the weave of the world emerge once more. The strings appeared more quickly this time, shimmering strands of silver and shadow and hues of green from the forest. All life was woven together and Zoe wondered how much she could manipulate these filaments, creating new things. Perhaps destroying them, too.

A crack in the forest. The snap of a branch.

Zoe sat up sharply and peered around at the thick trees, suddenly less of a haven and more a forbidding place of hard wood and sharp spines.

She looked down at the sleeping Mapwalker team. They were all exhausted, slumbering deeply. She didn't want to wake them and it was most likely one of the forest creatures going about its nightly hunt. She was just jumpy. There was nothing to worry about.

But as she turned back, a flash of silver caught the moonlight. A shadowy figure loomed over her. She opened her mouth to scream a warning, but a sharp pain at her temple turned everything black.

* * *

A chorus of birdsong woke Sienna as the sky turned from inky blue to pastel shades, the stars fading as light returned to the forest. She had slept all night and missed her turn at the watch. For a moment, she was grateful for it. Her body had regained its strength, and the creatures of the cavern were only a memory now they were out in the fresh air. But someone else must have taken her turn.

She sat up, noting that Mila and Perry were only just waking up beside her.

"Zoe," Sienna called up to the top of the rock. "Are you there?"

No answer. Just the call of birds warbling and whistling above.

Sienna rolled to her feet, unease rising within as she walked around the boulder and then clambered up onto it. Zoe was nowhere to be seen, her pack left discarded on the top of the rock.

Mila sat up and rubbed her eyes. "What is it? Did we sleep through?"

Sienna jumped down, pack in hand. "Zoe's not here."

"I'm sure she's just in the trees somewhere. She can't have gone far." Perry got to his feet, shaking sleep from his limbs, and clambered up the rock. "Zoe!"

Birds flew from the treetops at his cry, winging across the ever-lightening sky toward the jagged peaks beyond. But there was no answering call, no footsteps from the forest.

Perry pointed to a gap in the trees. "What's that? It looks different from last night."

Sienna jogged over to where the treeline parted into a semblance of a path, Mila and Perry right behind her. The carefully piled cairn of stones was now strewn across the track and next to it, a huge footprint in the dust.

"What is that?" Perry hunkered down to look more closely. "It's more animal than human but like nothing I've seen before."

Sienna's stomach turned at the sight of it. They had not left the Shadow behind in the cave system. Perhaps their use of magic had even alerted whatever ruled this area of the Borderlands. Whatever it was, it had Zoe.

CHAPTER 13

SIENNA CROUCHED BY MILA as they examined the footprint more carefully. "It could be a mutant," Mila said. "One of those bred by the Shadow Cartographers. But why take Zoe?"

Perry stood and looked down the path, his face etched with concern. "It doesn't matter why. We have to go after her. We can track it, follow its path."

Mila shook her head. "We have to get to the Tower of the Winds. Our mission is to help Bridget re-open the border. Every moment we delay, Earthside suffers further. Zoe knew the risks when she—"

"No," Sienna cut in sharply. "We go after Zoe. We need her." She stood and spun on her heel, walking back to where the packs lay, her face flushed as she thought of the Weaver. The way ahead wasn't clear, but she knew Zoe was important somehow. And besides, they couldn't leave her in the camp of the mutants. Sienna thought back to Xander's end, sucked dry of his magic and life force by the coldly beautiful Elf. She would not leave another of the team to die so far from home.

Sienna picked up her pack. "We need to get going. They're hours ahead of us already."

"I hope you know what you're doing," Mila said, shaking her head as she grabbed her pack.

Perry snatched his up, shouldering Zoe's as well and strode into the forest.

Together they walked under the trees as morning light broke through the canopy, dappling the way ahead. The path wound past thick trunks, torchwood and ebony amongst them, hard tropical trees no longer so densely packed on Earthside, cleared for timber and other crops. Sienna spotted orchids as they walked by, bright colors of purple and scarlet, a glimpse of beauty in a dangerous land.

She had heard of the camp of the mutants, new species cultivated by the Shadow Cartographers, bred from humans with different magical powers to enable new strains to emerge. She remembered the Fertility Halls in the Castle of the Shadow, Finn's face as his sister died in his arms, his niece taken for the cause. She wondered where he was now, whether he thought of her at all. Finn had made it clear that his path lay in the Borderlands, whereas her allegiance would always be to Earthside. She had thought they could somehow make a future together, but it seemed impossible right now.

The forest path emerged at the base of a rock face pitted with fissures as if gouged by giant talons. Jagged peaks spiked into the sky toward the sun. It burned hot now they were out of the shade of the forest, the air more humid. Sienna wiped her brow of sweat as she searched for the way ahead.

She had a sense of time ticking down to some imagined countdown, when Earthside would crumple into the hard border, triggering an unstoppable series of natural disasters that would devastate her home. Yet being here shifted her perspective and made her wonder whether it was time for such a dramatic change in fortunes. Time for a new power to rise.

Sienna shook her head, banishing the thought that seemed to come from nowhere. Her skin burned under her t-shirt, and she sensed the whorls of shadow spinning ever faster. Was she transforming now she grew closer to the source?

"Are you okay?" Mila asked, putting a hand on Sienna's arm.

Sienna gave a faint smile. "Just over-heating, I guess." She pointed ahead. "We need to hurry. I don't think we have much time."

* * *

Zoe woke to a jolting rhythm, a bump-bump stride that jerked her into consciousness. She half-wondered why the rock beneath her moved, then remembered the shadowy figure looming above before all went black. She opened her eyes and froze as she looked up at the thing that carried her.

A craggy face with skin cracked like dried mud, muscles heaped like sacks of rock under a tunic stretched tight over its colossal body. It smelled like moss and minerals leaching from a mountain stream. As Zoe shifted, it stopped walking and looked down at her. Something like a smile crossed its face, a wide mouth opening like a cleft in stone, eyes like tiny emeralds hidden in the crevices.

"He likes you."

Zoe turned in the creature's arms to see a young girl, perhaps ten years old, blonde hair in messy plaits tied with twine, wearing a tunic the color of ripe olives. She signed with her hands and the living rock placed Zoe gently on the ground. She found her legs a little unsteady, and it held an arm out for her to lean against. There was consideration in the gesture, but Zoe understood that its docile manner would change if she tried to run. She glanced around at the high cliffs surrounding them, serrated edges like flint knives spiked with cactus and thorny scrub. There was nowhere to run to, anyway.

The girl approached and examined Zoe, looking her up and down with a maturity far beyond her age. "You have a strange aura. I've never sensed it before. What magic can you do?"

Zoe frowned. "You can sense magic?"

The girl nodded. "I see colors and textures around those with ability and I can usually tell what they can do. We're scouts, me and Hashim." She reached out a small hand and stroked the creature's arm. It was a familiar gesture, a touch of connection between friends. But as much as Zoe found these two fascinating, she had to figure out a way to get back to the Mapwalker team.

"Who are you scouting for?"

The girl looked puzzled. "Who else? The silver-haired one and the old man. They offer good coin for such as you. We need to take supplies back for my family and your trade will mean we can return with food." Her eyes darted away. "Maybe even medicine. My little brother …"

As her words trailed off, Zoe wondered how it was possible that this young girl was the only way her family could get the supplies they needed. It was a glimpse into a side of the Borderlands she had never appreciated before. This was not some utopian world of magic and plenty. It was a land of desperately poor people ruled by an upper class of Shadow Cartographers whose obsession with reclaiming Earthside reduced all to poverty. If they would only spend their energy building and improving what they had, this side of the border could prosper.

"I sensed there were others with you," the girl continued. "Maybe one with greater power than yours, but I have seen her kind before. I've seen no one like you." She came closer, this time reaching out a hand to caress the air around Zoe's face, like a blind girl reading features with touch. "It's beautiful."

Zoe didn't sense any danger from the pair and yet she

knew their destination might lead to her end. They might not know what happened to those they delivered up — or they chose to ignore it — but Zoe understood loyalty to family above all else. Perhaps she would do the same in their position.

She shifted her vision to examine the strings of the world around, allowing the weave of nature to come into focus. After the cave, she knew her magic was strong enough to manipulate the strands. She could trap these two and then escape into the labyrinth of rocks — but the use of magic would sap her energy and exchange drops of shadow for its use, the toll greater if used here in the Borderlands. The Mapwalker team would surely look for her once they woke and would come in this direction. She would bide her time for now and wait a little longer.

"I'm a Weaver. My name is Zoe."

The girl's eyes widened. "A Weaver. Oh, my. You're worth so much." She skipped around in a tight circle, plaits flying, dancing with joy as she beamed with pleasure. The rocky hulk of Hashim shook and then a booming laugh rang out at his friend's delight. Zoe couldn't help but join in, giggling a little at the strange scene, even as she questioned why the hell she might be so valuable.

The girl stopped spinning. "I'm Callen." She held out a hand. "Pleased to meet you, Weaver Zoe."

Zoe shook her hand with appropriate solemnity, wondering if the pair treated all their captives so well.

Callen turned suddenly, looking back into the forest, as if hearing a far-off sound. "We need to get moving. Your friends are on the trail, but we will trade well before they arrive."

Zoe hadn't realized they were so close to the camp. She had to get away.

She raised her hands, focusing on the strands of light and shadow — but the giant Hashim folded his bulky arms around her, crushing her to his chest. She couldn't move, could barely breathe.

Callen stepped in closer, transformed from a charming little girl to the steely eyed bounty hunter once more.

"You don't have to do this," Zoe gasped. "I can help your family. Please don't—"

Hashim squeezed more tightly, cutting off her pleas.

Callen remained silent as she clambered up onto Hashim's back, riding his shoulders as if they were one creature, a strange pairing in a land of aberration.

The mutant lifted Zoe up, locking her into a vice of stone. He stood and strode on past the towering cliffs, each stride ten times that of a man. Zoe knew that the Mapwalker team would never reach her in time. She would face the mutant camp alone.

CHAPTER 14

"IT'S NOT FAR NOW." Titus pointed to the flank of the mountain, the blush of dawn painting it in shades of coral and amber. "The munitions dump is on the edge there, near the snow line to keep it cool and away from the major trade routes."

Finn hunkered down on a log and made a small fire, boiling up water for coffee while they both ate in silence from the supplies of meat and bread that Kabila had given them. Both men were used to marching on military rations, so they ate quickly and before long, they were heading up the side of the mountain.

Titus scanned the rocky escarpment above, pointing out features of the slope. "It's between three points — the summit, the woman's profile, and a dead tree struck by lightning. The cache is equidistant from each."

They zigzagged up the side, navigating the scree and patches of scrub where tiny wild flowers grew, purple against green. Finn found his breath ragged as they climbed, the slope becoming ever steeper.

Finally, a dead tree came into view, its stark white limbs reaching for blue sky as the sun burned down upon them. Titus turned to scan the surrounding area, then pointed at a rocky outcrop a little higher and to the east. "There."

Finn supposed it could be a woman's profile at a stretch, but Titus seemed sure and set off to climb higher, picking up his pace as they neared their goal. Finn turned to look back over the plain. They were high above the forest line now and below, the trader town stretched to the coastline, the sea shimmering beyond to the horizon. It looked so peaceful from up here, with no sense of the suffering that lay within its streets. But as much as this wild place had a stark beauty, Finn was a city boy, and his life blood beat to the pulse of a faster pace of life. If he survived this mission, he would return to Old Aleppo and liberate it from the iron grip of his father. Perhaps Sienna would even join him and they would eat oranges together in the market in a time of peace.

He shook his head and gave a rueful laugh. If only life could be so simple.

"Come and help me!" Titus shouted down from higher up. He was on his knees by a thorn bush, scrabbling at the ground.

Finn hurried up the slope and together, they cleared the rocks and dug down into the ground beneath.

"There should be enough explosives in here to destroy the main crop." Titus grinned in anticipation at what they would find. "It's been way too long since I've done some proper demolition, but I'm sure I'll get back into the swing of it."

They soon hit upon a metal trunk and as the sun rose high overhead, they levered the lid open and revealed what lay within.

Finn sat back on the hard ground, staring into the chest with despair. It was completely filled with rocks, hiding the fact that the explosives had been taken long ago.

Titus picked up one of the stones and hurled it down the slope with a violent shout. He picked up another, then another, throwing until he exhausted his frustration.

"We'll go on anyway," Finn said. "We don't know what

we'll find at the camp. Maybe fertilizer you can use. There will surely be something explosive."

Titus sat down heavily and sighed. "You're right. I just hoped this would give us some advantage. It's the two of us against whatever is out there. We have no chance."

Finn pulled out a flask of water and took a sip before passing it over to Titus. "There's always a chance. Besides, what else do you want to do now? We can at least scout the camp and if it's impossible to destroy the crop, we'll return to the Resistance for reinforcements." He pointed back to the trader town. "Think of all the people down there taking Liberation, addicts getting their fix, women carrying monsters. Every day that drug is loose it corrupts more Borderlanders and turns them to the Shadow."

"Or leaves them dead in its wake," Titus said quietly. "So we go on." He pointed up the face of the mountain. "It's faster to go up and over than around at lower altitude. If the weather holds, that is. The forest lower down ends in towering pinnacles of rock and a labyrinth of stone needles. It's hard to navigate. If we descend from above, we can at least figure out the best way into the camp."

They both stood and brushed down their clothes, then set off up the mountain, faces set toward the peak, footsteps even, breath panting as they rose higher.

To be honest, Finn had never wanted to climb a mountain and after this experience, he never wanted to climb one again. Titus kept up a grueling pace from years of experience on this kind of terrain, but Finn felt every single step of the hard ground, his leg muscles screaming in pain as they wound their way up toward the peak.

The weather held, sun baking down on them with no shelter from the heat even as the wind whipped their faces. But each step took them closer to the camp, so Finn gritted his teeth and kept walking.

Just another ten paces.

And another ten.

Finally, they skirted the summit in a haze of clouds, the valley before them obscured in mist. But Finn felt a change in the air and sensed a kind of shimmer in the gloom beyond. The way down was even harder on his leg muscles and his knees ached with every jolt on the rocky ground.

As they descended, the mist cleared, and the sun came out again. Suddenly, they saw the camp laid out below them.

A wide lake lay in the center with organized barracks, and before it, a central plaza with some kind of temple. Further out, a patchwork of crops in shades of green and fields of blue.

"All different stages of growth," Titus said. "They've got a year-round crop here. Enough to dose the whole of the Borderlands."

Finn marveled at the scope of the Liberation project, the drug an effective route to the ultimate goal of creating a superhuman army to take back Earthside. His father, the Warlord, Kosai, was a man of great cruelty with no love for Earthsiders, but Finn doubted that even he would countenance dosing his own people with such a drug. This was masterminded by those closely aligned with the Shadow.

Resolve hardened within him as they descended into the valley. Finn would not leave this place without burning those crops down.

As they approached the fields, they stopped behind a rocky outcrop to plan the next step. Workers tended the plants, immigrant slaves amongst the crops, while Shadow Guards patrolled the perimeter. The balmy evening made the guards relaxed and lazy, and at some command posts, they played cards and joked with each other. Clearly, tending fields was not a high-stress position, and they were not concerned about possible attack.

Piles of fertilizer lay at specific points amongst the fields and workers occasionally went into huts, so perhaps more lay within. It was peaceful, a deadly beauty with a malignant harvest. But as Finn watched the pastoral scene play out down below, he knew they couldn't possibly destroy this entire crop. They didn't have enough people to start fires at the same time, and both he and Titus would likely be caught trying to set the fields alight alone.

It was an impossible mission.

CHAPTER 15

ZOE SMELLED THE CAMP before she saw it, a stench of too many people, cooking fires and the faint metallic scent left after an electrical storm, the residue of spent magic. Hashim had carried her for several hours, Callen on his back, never slowing, never stopping until they reached the end of the tangle of paths through the rocky chasm and emerged at the edge of a valley.

A river ran down from the mountains into a vast lake with a church submerged in the middle, perhaps drowned on Earthside and pushed through here by lack of belief. There were fields of some kind of crop with blue flowers in vast terraces up the slope, workers moving in channels between them.

Around the lake, the camp was divided into clear sections, more like military barracks than the ramshackle place Zoe had imagined. There were permanent structures built at strategic positions around the edge and open training grounds where groups of soldiers marched in formation. The sound of laughter echoed up from children out at play in a schoolyard. It looked just like any other small town—

A flash of blue light above a temple by the side of the lake.

The soldiers stopped marching. The children fell silent. Even the birds muted their song. Hashim and Callen froze, eyes fixed on the scene.

The light rose like a mushroom cloud from the vaulted roof and then dissipated into haze.

Zoe felt the tension drain from her captors as all evidence of the light disappeared.

"Let's go," Callen said. "It's a good time to trade." The girl's voice trembled a little, as if she had to convince herself to go on.

Hashim walked into the valley. He stepped more carefully now, covering the ground a little slower as he dodged the boulders on the way down.

"Why is it a good time to trade?" Zoe asked. "What was that light?"

Callen was silent a moment and then spoke softly. "They always need more resources after they use someone up." She looked down at the ground, her young face haunted. "They say it doesn't hurt when they take your magic. They say it's quick …" Her words trailed off, her gaze fixed on the camp ahead.

They soon reached the perimeter where two guards with the half-moon tattoo of the Warlord waved them through, clearly recognizing Callen and her strange partner. But as they moved into the camp itself, Zoe saw that Hashim was not so strange after all.

The path led directly toward the temple cut across by concentric circular routes that linked each area. Hashim or his kind were clearly unremarkable as no one gave him a second glance as they walked through, although Zoe noted a few people looked up at her with interest. A pair of twins, long-limbed with black skin and curious eyes, ran past and circled back for a second look. But no one challenged or even spoke to them. Guards on patrol walked by at regular intervals, keeping a tight grip on security.

Hashim strode down through the camp until they reached the back of the temple where two guards stood either side of a staircase that led up to a finely carved wooden door. As they approached, one guard ran up the stairs and knocked twice, then once again.

The door opened an inch and Zoe glimpsed a swirl of shadow inside and a hand with bony fingers. She felt eyes upon her, a chill creeping up her spine as if she had been plunged under ice, drowning in the depths under a thick layer of impenetrable blue.

The figure dropped back into darkness; the door left ajar.

The guard stepped forward to meet Hashim. Callen jumped down, her demeanor one of a trader far beyond her years.

"He'll take this one." The guard pulled a leather pouch of coins from his belt and handed it to Callen. She opened it, her eyes widening in appreciation. "And he'll take any more like her you can find."

Callen wouldn't meet Zoe's eyes as Hashim placed her gently on the ground. The giant patted her head in a friendly manner. He clearly did not understand what part he played in the demise of so many who carried magic in their veins.

Callen clambered up onto his shoulders and without even looking back, they began the long climb out of the camp.

The guard grabbed Zoe's arm and thrust her up the stairs toward the door.

"Please," she begged. "Don't do this."

The guard didn't acknowledge her words and as the door opened wider; he pushed her forward and darted away down the stairs without even a glance back.

Zoe stumbled inside the darkened room and blinked as her eyes adjusted to the dim light. It was starkly beautiful, like a forest transformed into architecture. Thick pillars of cedar wood stretched from the floor carved with vines and the faces of mutated woodland creatures, twisted into visages of horror. The delicate smell of cedar pervaded the space, refreshing and cool after the hot exterior. Oak beams stretched up into a coffered ceiling painted in shades of midnight and on the side facing the lake, an arched window stood covered by thick drapes. A sliver of light lanced across the wooden floor, empty except for a single chair — and the man who stood in the shadows behind it.

"You're a Weaver." His voice held the kind of interest that a predator has in a particularly tasty prey.

He walked toward her, avoiding the ray of light on the ground, and it seemed as if he merely skimmed the earth. Zoe blinked once more to try to focus on his figure, but his outline constantly shifted, as if smoke wreathed his flesh. She caught her breath as she realized this man was almost a creature of pure shadow. She had read of these powerful Mapwalkers who turned, but she had never wished to meet one.

He came closer, distinguished features betraying his nobility on Earthside and an old facial scar evidence of past battles.

"I'm Sir Douglas Mercator. What's your name?"

"Zoe." She blurted it out quickly, then clapped a hand over her mouth. It had been a reflex, a polite response to an unremarkable question, but she had totally failed interrogation 101.

Sir Douglas laughed. "Oh, don't worry. You're safe with me." He glanced toward the door to the lakeside. "At least for now. Come. Sit. You have nowhere else to be." He pointed at the chair.

Zoe's heart beat faster as she walked across the floor and sat, straight-backed. She needed to stall for time because there was no easy way out of here. Guards stood outside the doors and in here, a Shadow Cartographer who could wrap her in shadow weave or crush her lungs with a wave of his hand.

"How did you get here?"

"The bounty-hunter girl, Callen, and her giant friend, found me lost in the forest."

Sir Douglas took a step forward. "Try again. How did you get into the Borderlands? The border is closed and none have passed through it since the Ministry slammed it shut, damning us all." His features contorted with rage as he spat the final words.

He bent down until his angular nose almost touched hers and gripped her chin hard, turning her face up toward him. His grey eyes were the color of a wolf pelt, an old alpha male with sharp teeth covered in the blood of its prey.

"Tell me."

Zoe thought of her desk back at the Ministry, the calm, quiet atmosphere of the Antiquities department. She should have just stayed down there and told no one of what she had seen. Bridget had not prepared her for any of this. She was just a Weaver, after all, but she had to tell him something.

"We came through a path of the dead, one of the ancient Egyptian tombs full of creatures and traps and—"

"We?" Sir Douglas snarled as he cut off her words.

Zoe bit her lip as she realized her mistake, but she wouldn't give her friends up. Whatever he did to her.

Sir Douglas turned away, his robes a swirl of smoke. He strode across the floor, shaking his head as if deeply troubled. "The way has only been used in rare times," he muttered. "It cannot be crossed without …" He spun around. "A powerful Blood Mapwalker. You came with Sienna Farren. Perhaps he is with her …" Sir Douglas's voice trailed off and Zoe thought she saw something wistful in his gaze, an edge of vulnerability.

The door from the front of the temple banged open and his eyes turned cold once more, like a graveyard as storm clouds gathered overhead. The sound of a growing crowd came from outside, cheers of excitement mingling with the anticipation of carnival pleasure.

A young woman with pixie features entered, her silver hair reflecting the sun from outside, a white dress swirling around her slight figure. This must be Elf, but even though Sienna had described her, somehow, the girl was smaller than she expected.

"Oh, wonderful. You found me a fresh one. We just have time before the challenge." Elf reached out a hand.

Zoe felt a jerk inside, as if the girl reached inside her chest to tug on her heart. Her ribcage contracted and suddenly, she couldn't breathe. Something — her magic — seeped from her in tiny pulses. Like the death of a thousand cuts, Elf would drain her dry.

Zoe gasped for breath, tears running down her cheeks as she doubled over, clutching her hands to her aching chest.

Sir Douglas stepped in between them and the pain stopped. "Not yet," he said sharply. "She came with others more powerful. We need to know more."

Elf spun on her heel, her face like thunder as she marched to the window and threw back the drapes, letting light flood into the temple. Sir Douglas shrank back into the shadows, but not before Zoe saw the smoke at the edge of his robes disappearing in the sun, evaporating like clouds on a summer day.

The window had a view out over the vast lake and the ruined church at its center. Four huge vats of a deep blue liquid sat directly in front on the shore.

"She is enough for this batch of Liberation. You can't stop me." Elf turned around again and raised her hand. Zoe shrank back, waiting for the pain once more. They were both in sunlight now and Sir Douglas could not stop her again.

"Sienna came over the border," he said from the shadows.

Elf frowned and dropped her hand. "How? The border is closed." She shook her head, eyes narrowing in concern. "No matter. Her blood is the key. If I can siphon it at the Tower of the Winds, I can amplify my power and smash down the border for good. Earthside will be ours for the taking." She smiled triumphantly. "Where is she?"

Sir Douglas circled the edge of the temple, staying out of the light. "I was just about to find out. But your magic is of no use for — persuasion. Give me more time. I will find her."

Elf smiled in anticipation. "Then I will take whatever you leave behind of this one when you're finished." A cheer rose up from outside. "But hurry, the challenge begins soon."

She pulled the drapes closed, leaving the room in semi-darkness again, and swept out the door. Zoe watched her go, icy fear creeping through her veins as Sir Douglas circled behind her.

Chill fingers touched her neck, gently brushing her hair to one side.

"Tell me where they are," he whispered, the threat clear as his grip tightened, bone digging into flesh as if he might burrow within her.

CHAPTER 16

FORBIDDING SHARDS OF ROCK loomed above the Mapwalker team as they wound through the labyrinth of paths below the jagged peaks. Sienna no longer knew how she chose the forks ahead, only trusting that the pulse of shadow inside drew her on to her fate. It felt symbiotic now, a separate presence inside her, but one that belonged there. She couldn't talk about it with the others and she wondered whether all those who ended up in a shadow coma felt this way before succumbing to the darkness. Whatever it was, it pulled her on.

They reached the end of the path in the balmy early evening. A gentle breeze wafted over the valley before them as they crouched in the lee of a pile of boulders and looked out over the camp.

"It's huge," Perry said. "More like a small city. How will we find her?"

"And get out of there alive," Mila added. She tilted her head to one side as she stared down at the lake. "What is that?"

Within the blue waters, an electric storm churned, crackles of energy radiating out from thick serpentine bodies. They writhed together, then raced around the sunken church at the center.

"They look like electric eels but they must be gigantic."

Mila sounded both fascinated and appalled at the same time, and Sienna wondered if her friend longed to sink into those cool waters. Perhaps she understood the dichotomy of both longing for the Shadow and fighting against it? She remembered Mila's face in the caves under Ganvié as she left Ekon behind to finish the mission. Perhaps they both had regrets about what — and who — they had left behind.

A cry rang out overhead, a sound of desperate loss with a distinctly human quality. Sienna looked up to see the silhouette of a giant creature against the clouds, its body some kind of hybrid bird, its wings like monstrous sails criss-crossed with bones of human anatomy, talons like razor blades hanging below. She shuddered and looked away. She didn't want to see its face, didn't want to imagine how they could have created such a beast. It cried out again and winged its way across the valley, heading out over the lake.

"We need to get moving. We can't leave Zoe here any longer." Sienna tamped down the rising fear as she watched the creature fly away.

On Earthside, the theory of eugenics involved breeding the best of a species to create superior beings. But the dark side of the practice involved killing those considered inferior by the ruling class, no matter their true worth. Here in the Borderlands, they had taken the philosophy to extremes, breeding whatever they could in terms of magical ability and physical deformity with the aim of creating an overwhelming force that could take back the land they believed was rightfully theirs. If they were too late, Zoe would be the latest victim in an endless bloody war.

They walked down the side of the valley as quickly as they could over the rocky ground, approaching the camp from an oblique angle and staying away from the main entrance which bristled with guards. A rubbish tip spilled out from the side of the camp toward the cliff face, a deep crevice scarring the rock face behind.

Sienna pointed up to it as they approached. "If anything happens, if we get separated, we meet there. Wait one sunset and one sunrise." She hesitated a moment. "Then leave."

Perry and Mila both nodded and Sienna could only hope that they would all walk out of the camp together with Zoe by their side.

The stench of waste greeted them as they reached the edge of the tip, rotting produce underpinned by a copper tang of butchered flesh and spilled blood. Perry pulled up his t-shirt, holding it against his mouth and nose. Sienna tried to breathe shallowly through her mouth, but nothing kept the awful stink from them. At least it kept the guards away from this area and only a few scrawny children sifting through the rubbish at the edge of the tip witnessed their arrival, skeletal frames on the edge of survival unheeding of the passers-by.

Mila clambered up the pile of rubbish to where it spilled over a wall into the camp, Sienna and Perry close behind her. They dropped down into a warren of ramshackle shelters and weather-worn tents fortified by sheets of metal and planks of wood.

Like all shanty towns, this one was filled with desperate people, working however they could to feed their children. With no magic, they were worthless to the Shadow Cartographers, used only for manual labor in the mines and camps. Were they also used as pure life energy, transformed into darkness by the silver-haired Elf?

Grief jolted through Sienna as she remembered those terrifying last moments as Elf sucked the life from Xander and his lion, Asada, using it to power the infection and transformation of the mutant plague rats. Sienna had no direct evidence that the girl was here, but she sensed the presence of a powerful Shadow Cartographer, one who commanded the camp and directed the metamorphosis of the creatures within.

An old woman peered out from behind a ragged curtain, her features etched with deep lines betraying her years of suffering. She looked at them with bleary eyes, a flicker of interest quickly dying as they passed by.

The team walked in silence, alert for any sign of danger, but the streets seemed oddly deserted as they skirted a path leading downhill toward the lakeside.

The sounds of a crowd soon came from up ahead. There was a sense of excitement and festivity in the air, incongruous in a place that seemed so full of desperation.

A slow drumbeat began, booming out across the valley.

Perry shook his head and sighed. "Nothing good happens when the drum starts."

Sienna knew what he meant. They had heard the drums at the Tophet, the Warlord's place of child sacrifice, and again at the eyrie where Perry almost had his liver devoured by giant eagles.

The drum was the sound of death.

They ran toward it.

* * *

The drumbeat startled Finn, a sudden interruption to his concentrated study of the valley below.

Workers in the fields stopped pruning the plants and stood up to rub their backs and ease aches and pains. The guards gestured down the hill, giving permission to stop working. Groups of laborers set off toward the plaza, laughing together with a sudden sense of celebration.

Finn followed the lines of the paths as they walked down the slopes to the barracks at the bottom, neatly organized in ranks with dirt tracks between.

In the center of the camp, an open plaza lay in front of a lake with a sunken church at its heart. Finn could just make out black shadows undulating within the depths and he shuddered to think what monsters lay below the surface.

A sizeable building — a temple of some kind — stood in front of the lake and behind it, by the water's edge, sat deep vats of inky blue liquid. Finn narrowed his eyes as he focused on the unusual feature. Then he realized what they must be.

A great deal of water would be needed to turn the plant extract into liquid doses of Liberation that could be bottled and distributed. Someone needed to add the twisted magic to the belladonna before it was shipped and it made sense to store it centrally.

Finn pointed to the pools of blue. "We destroy those and it will disrupt the entire supply chain, at least for a time. Then we bring others from the Resistance to help finish the place."

Titus nodded and pointed at a roughly hewn hut on the edge of the plaza with more guards than the rest. "I'd say that's where they keep weapons, maybe explosives. We should duck in there on the way down."

The drum beat faster, its rhythm steadily increasing.

Finn stood up. "Come on. This is our chance. We'll join the workers and mingle with the crowd." He set off at a run down the hill between rows of deadly plants, Titus right behind. They tagged along at the back of a group of farmhands, laughing and joking as if they had come from plantations higher up the mountain.

"Good day for a sacrifice," one man said. "Helps the crops grow faster, see. Goddess be praised."

Finn nodded, the words bringing back memories of his father's sacrifices at the Tophet. Blood always drew a crowd. He pitied the victim, but the distraction would be perfect. He and Titus could proceed with their plan unseen.

As the crowd streamed into the plaza, they peeled off, skirting the edge of the barracks and circling around to the back of the guard's hut. Constructed of wood and raised on stilts, the hut had a 360 degree walkway around the perimeter and a central staircase up the middle. One way in, one way out.

Heavily armed guards walked the perimeter, but as the drum beat faster, those at the back edged forward so they could see the action.

Finn and Titus ducked underneath the walkway and ran to the staircase. The boom of the drum grew louder and faster, the resonance so deep it made Finn's heart beat in time. A neat trick to fire up the crowd and make the soldiers above want to join the party. He could only hope they stayed distracted.

Finn pulled his sword and ran up the stairs on light feet, eyes darting around for any guards. No one in sight. He beckoned Titus up and stood watch while the explosives expert ducked inside the building, leaving the door ajar as he searched for something they could use.

Seconds passed, and Finn counted his breaths. He stood motionless, listening for footsteps under the drum beat, but the soldiers stayed riveted to the scene in the plaza.

Then the drumbeat stopped.

A rustle inside and then silence as Titus must have frozen in his search, aware that the soldiers were only meters away.

The crowd erupted into a cheer, their shouts and applause a deafening roar.

Titus ducked out the hut, bag in hand, triumphant grin on his face. He ran down the steps and Finn dashed after him with no fear of being heard under the sound of celebration. They kept moving until they were well away from the guard's hut.

Behind one of the barracks, Titus stopped and opened his bag. Sticks of dynamite used for mining rock and a long roll of detonator cord lay inside. "I only wish I could have taken more."

Finn looked back at the raucous crowd. Working Borderlanders, some mutated, but most here as slaves.

"We should try to minimize the damage and only blow the Liberation vats. Maybe bring down that temple on whatever dark power is inside." He pointed at the building. "We just need to get around the back. We'll rig explosives while the crowd is fixated on whatever the hell is happening out there."

They ran on, skirting the edge of the crowd as a carnival atmosphere took hold. Couples reveled in the shadows, so engaged with each other that Finn and Titus passed unnoticed.

Four huge vats stood on the edge of the lake, giant wooden structures made from aged oak on tall stilts with lines of taps underneath for the bottling process. A ladder up one side led to a series of walkways between them.

Titus pointed up. "Take the detonator cord and wind it between the vats, then drop it down. I'll set the explosives underneath and then connect it together. Hurry now, we're running out of time."

CHAPTER 17

MILA PULLED AHEAD OF Perry and Sienna as the path narrowed on the hill, switch-backing between the shanty town structures to emerge between military style barracks. People thronged the street, heading down toward the central area. Street vendors hawked their wares in a carnival atmosphere, the smell of roasted nuts mingling with hops as revelers drank ale from barrels. Mila slowed down to walk next to a buxom young woman, who swayed a little as she swigged from a pewter mug.

"This should be exciting," Mila said, smiling in welcome.

"Oh yes," the woman said. "We haven't had such as these for a while. Some say they're true aberrations, powerful enough to make it through the challenge." She gave a sly grin. "But it will go better for me if they're ravaged or devoured."

Her words startled Mila with their violent intent, but she kept a smile plastered on her face. "Why's that?"

The woman thrust her ample figure forward. "Good for business. The soldiers spend more coin after savagery." She laughed and took another swig.

Mila fell back to walk alongside Sienna and Perry. "There's some kind of competition or tournament and it might not end well for whoever's involved."

"Do you think it's Zoe?" Perry asked with a frown of concern.

"Perhaps, but the woman mentioned 'they' as if there are multiple contenders. We have to get closer."

Mila wiggled through the crowd, flowing with the stream of people until she reached a low wall at the water's edge with a clear view. A ceremonial temple made from thick wooden pillars carved with magical symbols stood pride of place and before it, a wide open plaza. The sense of excitement was palpable, a thrum of energy from the gathered masses, eager for blood.

A flash of blue light came from out on the lake, then the buzz and snap of electrical force as something twisted toward the shore. It darted below the wall and Mila recognized its shape. An enormous electric eel, its body as thick as the wheel of a car, crackling with its own current. From the flashes of light further out, there were more of them waiting to be fed.

Sienna and Perry joined her by the wall as a hush fell over the crowd.

Two figures walked out from the wooden temple doorway, a silver-haired young girl with a willowy figure next to a tall man wrapped in a cloak of shadow, his face obscured by a hood. He stayed out of the sunlight, shielded by one of the pillars.

"Elf," Sienna whispered, and Mila remembered what her friend had told of Xander's death. The girl's power was not to be underestimated.

"And my father," Perry said, his voice hardening. "Or what's left of him."

Mila narrowed her eyes, trying to focus on the shape of Sir Douglas, but he was more a cloud of particles than a solid body now.

The transition to pure shadow was by all accounts a painful one, undertaken by only the most powerful Cartographers. It was unclear how much of the original man lay beneath that dusky blur, but while his physicality diminished, his magic grew.

These two were the central force powering the dark transformation of the Borderlands, and as the crowd cheered, raising their hands in salute, Mila wondered whether anyone could stop them.

Elf's sweet girlish voice rang out. "You are all welcome here tonight to witness the challenge. The reward for survival is great, but the risk is only undertaken by a chosen few." She pointed out to the lake. "Tonight, the challenge is something we have never seen before. A magic once thought lost has been reborn. If the challenge is won, we will have a new force to add to the army of the Borderlands."

She turned and beckoned to the side of the dais.

Two slight figures walked onto the stage, their steps hesitant as they emerged in front of the crowd.

Mila gasped at the sight of them. Twins with skin as black as Ekon's, limbs as long and slender as her own. A boy and a girl, twins, around eight or nine years old.

"Waterwalkers," Elf announced in triumph. "The first in a generation. They will face the challenge together." She pointed to the sunken church, its spire jutting out toward the night sky with a half-moon pennant flying from its peak. "Retrieve the flag and I will grant you the highest honor."

"They're only children," Sienna said softly. "How will they survive alone?"

Mila couldn't speak, could hardly breathe. She had thought for so long that she was the only one of her kind until she had met Ekon at Ganvié and seen evidence of their once great people. Now two more stood before her — about to go to their deaths.

Even if the children survived the electric eels, she didn't like the sound of the 'highest honor.' The challenge was clearly a way to find those who had the strongest magic, but what was their fate if they proved themselves?

The crowd parted before them as the children walked down the steps. There was no hesitation in their stride, their expressions determined as they faced the water. Waves lapped up on the shore, a surge generated by the powerful tails of the creatures below, their thick bodies undulating through the liquid, their blue light arcing out around them. The air hummed with anticipation as the twins reached the edge of the lake.

They stood for a moment on the shore, then dived in, bodies shimmering as they shifted into their magical form. The crowd gasped at the sight, unseen for so long.

Mila didn't hesitate.

She dived over the side of the wall into the water below, disappearing into the depths as she followed the Waterwalker twins.

* * *

Finn wound the explosive cord tightly around the barrels and then dropped it down through the center to Titus waiting below. As he emerged onto the walkway between the vats, he had an unobstructed view over the lake and the crowd beyond.

A splash caught his eye from the other side of the plaza where people gathered around a low wall.

Someone had dived in after the children.

Behind the wall, Finn saw the sun catch on bright titian hair before the figure ducked away into the crowd. Could it be Sienna? Was Mila the unknown swimmer?

His mind raced with the possibility of what it might mean. He had to find her and there was only one place they would all be heading for. He turned to peer around the vat to the temple. Surely, the Mapwalker team would head there next.

CHAPTER 18

As Mila sank into the lake, her body changed and she moved as one with the water, scanning around her for the Waterwalker children and keeping an eye out for the electric eels.

Other strange creatures moved in the gloom, the pulsating mass of globular jellyfish, their insides glowing with a bilious light, disfigured tentacles hanging down to catch passing prey. Shoals of silver-sided fish darted past with misshapen heads and tumors bulging from their spines. Even the rocks on the lake bed were contorted, as if twisted by some primeval force into submission. Whatever they did in this camp, it affected the environment as well as the people.

A flash in the black water ahead.

As her vision adjusted, Mila could just make out the thick body of one creature as it darted after the twins. These were no ordinary beasts, but mutants created by the Shadow. They were gigantic, hunting with high-voltage pulses like a radar to locate their quarry before crushing it in their coils and activating the electric charge.

A scream echoed through the water. "Daniel!"

The cry for help galvanized Mila into action and she darted through the water, accelerating past the eel. It lunged, snapping its jaws, sending a pulse of electricity through her.

A searing jolt of pain and her limbs softened. For a moment, Mila thought she would sink to the bottom of the lake, a broken thing ready to be devoured.

The eel twisted its coils, whipping its tail at her.

Mila summoned her strength and rolled, corkscrewing down and away before it could catch her — then hurtled toward where the sound had come from.

The sunken church emerged from the gloom, its once majestic windows covered with green algae, its graveyard now home to crawling, creeping things with poisonous spines and probing tentacles.

An eel lay wrapped around one of the Waterwalkers, the girl, her face flitting between water and skin as the creature pulsed with electricity. Her crumpled body was limp, her eyes closed.

Her brother tried in vain to pull the coils of the beast away, screaming as he tried to help her. "Dawn, wake up! You need to get out of there. Please!"

Their language was a different dialect to the one Ekon had spoken with her in the ruined world under Ganvié, but Mila understood his desperation.

As the eel pulsed once more, she dived down, remembering Ekon's words when she lay trapped under the boulder in the ancient pyramid.

You are water. You cannot be pinned down. No rock can trap you.

And no eel either. These children had no one to teach them the ways of their people. But she could show them now.

Mila swept past Daniel, surprise flashing over his face as she eased herself between the coils next to Dawn. She wrapped her arms around the girl, whispering to her. "You are water. Nothing can trap you."

Dawn shifted a little, her eyes flickering as she registered the strange presence. Then the little girl wrapped her arms around Mila, clutching her as a child needing protection. Mila felt the frail body turn into pure liquid and made herself the same, dissolving out from under the coils of the eel.

She darted into the nave of the church, Daniel following close behind.

The eel swam after them, crashing into the stone doorway, its body too thick to enter. They were safe — for now.

"Who are you?" the boy demanded as Mila laid his sister down on one pew.

"A friend," Mila said. "A Waterwalker."

Daniel crossed his arms, a frown on his face. "They told us there are no others. We're special, our magic is unique."

Mila smiled. "You're definitely special, more than you know, but there *are* more of us. I have a friend, Ekon. He lives where our people have always lived." She smoothed a hand over Dawn's forehead as the girl stirred. "I hope you can meet him."

"But we live here," Daniel said. "Elf is our friend. She said there'll be a party if we can bring back the flag."

I bet she did, Mila thought. But she didn't want to frighten the children.

"Have any of your other friends had parties with Elf?"

Daniel's frown deepened. "Some said they were having one, but they didn't come back to school, so maybe they didn't pass their challenge …" His voice faded away.

Dawn opened her eyes and tried to sit up. Daniel rushed to her side as Mila helped the girl and together, they sat side by side on the pew in the church. Water eddied around them from the circling of the eels beyond the stone walls. The faint sound of carnival from the shore echoed through the water. Bread and circuses indeed. The masses kept at bay with alcohol and sacrifice. But Mila would not see these children suffer the same fate as Xander.

"Did you come from Atlantis to save us?" Dawn asked hesitantly, the words unfamiliar in her mouth. "They told us you were all dead."

Mila shook her head, wondering what else the children had been told of their heritage. "I'm not from Atlantis, at least not that I know of. But I am here to help you."

Dawn curled inward, pulling her legs up to her chest as she looked at the door of the church, illuminated by flashes of light outside. The eels battered the surrounding stone, seeking a way in. "I don't want to go back out there."

Mila put her arm around the girl and Dawn leaned in, snuggling up as if desperate for the contact. Daniel sat up straight a little way off, still wary. Mila's heart ached for them both, knowing full well that they couldn't stay in this sanctuary for long. They had to leave this place — but they did not have to return to the camp.

Daniel stood up. "I will get the flag. I'll wave to shore, make it clear we won. Then we can work out how to get back safely." He smiled at Mila. "Elf will be pleased to meet you, too. Maybe you can come to our party?"

Dawn reached out a hand to her brother. "No," she whispered. "You haven't seen what she does."

Daniel snatched his arm away. "What do you mean? Elf is our friend."

Dawn shook her head. "She steals magic, she sucks it from you. When Jenny went for her party—" She turned to Mila to explain. "Jenny was my second best friend. She could make anything grow really big, insects and plants and animals." Her face crumpled and tears ran down her cheeks. "I followed them, Daniel. I saw Elf pull something out of Jenny, like a magical spark, and she sank to the ground as if she was just empty skin." The little girl shuddered. "I couldn't run in case they saw me. I watched them sweep up her remains. She was dead, Daniel. Elf killed her."

"Why didn't you tell me before?"

Dawn sighed. "You wouldn't have believed me, and anyhow, we couldn't get away from her. If she found out I knew, she would have killed me, I know it."

The eel outside smashed its tail into the door of the church once more, this time dislodging chunks of stone. A cloud of dust swirled through the water.

Mila looked up as a crack split one pillar to the side of the entrance, a fissure running up into the arch, dislodging the keystone. Another thump as the creatures outside battered their sanctuary. They didn't have long before the entire place came down around them.

CHAPTER 19

WHEN MILA DIVED INTO the water, Sienna quickly took a step back. She pulled Perry away from the edge out of the line of sight from the main stage as people around them shouted and pointed in excitement.

"Another Waterwalker!"

It would only be minutes before the guards made it to this area of the crowd. They slipped into the mass of revelers, aware of suspicious stares as they retreated. Sienna slipped her arm around Perry's waist and he hugged her close to his side. They giggled and joked as they pushed through, trying not to draw attention. Just another pair of drunken young lovers on their way to find somewhere more private.

The crowd thinned out toward the barracks at the back of the plaza and they ducked behind one of the huts.

"What is she doing?" Perry whispered, his fists clenched in frustration. "Now they know we're here. What can she possibly hope to achieve?"

Sienna shook her head. "I don't know if she even considered her actions. She saw the children and went to help. We don't know how it feels to have her kind of magic. They are others like us, but she is—"

"A shifter," Perry finished for her, and Sienna heard resignation in his voice. "She belongs here, doesn't she?"

Sienna nodded. "Perhaps. But she might need our help to get the children out. We have to assume she'll go to the meeting place if she can. We'll get Zoe and wait for her at the cave."

Perry grinned. "Just like that?"

"Just like that." Sienna peered around the side of the barracks. "The crowd's attention is still on the water but the guards will be looking for us. Sir Douglas knows of Mila's gift. He must know we're here."

She looked toward the temple, its wooden beams over the ceremonial door urging her closer. An energy pulsed from within, something bound with stripes of shadow and flashes of light, a sickening mix that made her dizzy. Sienna closed her eyes, attraction and repulsion warring inside as the earth shifted beneath her. Nausea rose inside and she put her hand on the barracks wall to steady herself.

"You okay?" Perry asked.

Sienna nodded. "She's in there. I'm sure of it." Her heart thumped as she considered who else might be in there with Zoe, but they had no choice. The Weaver could not be left behind.

They darted between the huts, hiding as groups of guards ran past. Some revelers spilled out of the main plaza, drinking in groups around campfires as dusk turned to night. They shouted and sung together, drowning their miserable lives with cheap ale and the promise of human connection, even just for one evening.

As Sienna and Perry drew closer to the temple, the atmosphere changed. People clustered in groups to pray, prostrating themselves on the ground as they reached toward their imagined salvation. One woman beat herself with a flail tipped in glass, ripping open her tunic, blood flowing from her wounds and dripping onto the earth.

She swayed in ecstasy, her lips moving in a constant prayer. "Transform me, renew me, remake me."

This place was a magnet for those who desired to become one with the Shadow, who would knowingly give their life force to join with something beyond their understanding. Perhaps it was ever thus, Sienna thought. Was her own quest to the Tower of the Winds any different? Was she really going to save Earthside or did she pursue it because she needed to see whatever called in her nightmares? The promise of power and the threat of annihilation would be held in balance until the moment she stepped into that place.

She looked up at the temple looming ahead. They had to get there first.

"Where are they?" Elf's high-pitched peal of a voice came from the front of the building. "The children should have captured the flag by now. Get some guards out there on the water."

She was distracted by the scene on the lake. They had a chance to get inside.

* * *

Perry ducked around the back of the temple, Sienna close behind. Two guards stood either side of a staircase, their attention distracted as they talked amongst themselves, unaware of the threat approaching. Zoe was in there, he was sure of it, and the thought of what his father might do to her made him feel sick.

Perry made it within a few meters before the guards saw him, eyes widening as they opened their mouths to shout a warning. He opened his palms and fired two perfectly aimed fireballs — small enough to swallow, expanding into a fast-burning flare.

The guards slumped to the ground, helmets smoking from the heat within.

Perry crept up the steps, wood creaking under his feet,

the sound drowned out by the din of the celebratory crowd. He pushed open the door and slipped inside, hands raised at the ready. A dark blue flame flickered around his fingertips with barely restrained energy as Sienna followed him inside.

It was dark at first, and it took a second for Perry's eyes to adjust to the dim light.

Zoe sat tied to a chair, arms bound to her sides, her face bloody and bruised, head hanging down, maybe unconscious. Perry wanted to run to her, pull her into his arms — but by her side stood the insubstantial figure of his father, Sir Douglas Mercator, the once regal frame reduced to almost complete shadow.

Yet, he was stronger now than he had ever been in flesh.

"I've been expecting you." Sir Douglas stepped forward, although it seemed as if he glided more than walked across the floor. In the half-light of the lamps, Perry could see within the folds of his cloak to the shaded contours beneath. His body was almost completely gone, transformed into shadows that rippled and twisted in and out of what once been flesh.

Perry raised his hands, turned his palms up and summoned his flame into writhing balls of fire. He lifted his chin, eyes fixed on his father as he channeled his magic, intensifying the flame until it burned hot as molten lava.

He had trained for this moment, summoning his father's face in the practice rooms under Bath Abbey, slamming fire into that gaunt visage over and over until it splintered into ash. But now he was here, he felt a heaviness in his limbs, a resistance to the one task he had set himself.

His father drew closer. "Join us, my son. There is much opportunity for you here." He reached out a hand toward Perry's cheek, gentle fingers outstretched.

In his eyes, Perry saw a flicker of the man he had known as a child. The man who had taken him to the woods and shown him the gift of fire, encouraging him to use his power in secret, to keep his Halbrasse status quiet in case he was chosen to fight for causes he did not believe in. A principled man — who had now given his life to the Shadow.

Perry stepped back and raised his hands again, causing flames to rise in pillars before him.

"We're here for Zoe."

Sir Douglas waved a dismissive hand. A curl of shadow extended out from his reach to swirl under Zoe's chin, lifting her face toward them, her skin marred from a beating.

"She is nothing." He snapped the shadow back and her head dropped again.

Perry heard Sienna's sharp intake of breath, instinctively knew that she would go to her friend. In that moment, he saw the trap.

Sir Douglas had always and only wanted Sienna. Perry's own power was nothing compared to that of a Blood Mapwalker, one who could be twisted to true darkness.

Sienna ran forward.

Sir Douglas wheeled toward her and opened his arms wide. He summoned a great veil of shadow that billowed high and wide, filling the air with dust and ash and the stink of the grave, obscuring the room with shade.

"No!" Perry cried. He shot his flames into the cloud of darkness, momentarily illuminating Sienna as she ran from Sir Douglas toward Zoe, her arms outstretched. But his fire crashed down into the floor, extinguished by the weight of particles in the air.

The Shadow Cartographer loomed tall above Sienna, his skeletal form suddenly filled out, as if darkness expanded his frame into some hybrid creature that straddled the realms of man. He stretched his arms wide and gathered her to him, enveloping her in shadow, their bodies shimmering as something rose in the darkness beyond.

A corridor. A portal. Back to the Tower of the Winds.

He couldn't let his father take Sienna.

Perry bellowed in rage, summoning flames to surround his entire body. He ran, a burning torch, head down into the cloud of dust and tackled the fading figure of Sir Douglas.

The three of them fell to the floor, writhing in a pile of ash. Perry grabbed tight, wrapping his arms around his father's chest, his knees latched on to what was left of the man's legs. He called forth the flames within, burning hotter than he had ever tried to burn before.

His father writhed beneath him, moaning in pain. The sound echoed through his very soul, his heart almost bursting — and yet Perry would not let go.

As he thrashed in agony, Sir Douglas released Sienna, his grip loosening as his fingers crackled in the heat. She rolled away, hair singed, her clothes burning as she crawled along the floor, coughing and retching in the smoke.

She looked back at him and Perry saw horror in her eyes, a reflection of two entwined still-living corpses, burned flesh oozing together, becoming one in their inevitable end. She reached out a hand, shaking her head as she begged him to stop.

But Perry didn't want to stop. This was his mission, the task he had come to complete. There would be no better chance to end the Shadow Cartographer. Flames roared in his ears, blood pounding in his head as the temperature rose. He gripped his father tighter, summoning all the power he had left, determined to burn them out of existence together.

The door burst open.

Brilliant white light shot through the cloud of ash, as sharp as a blade, throwing Perry off his father.

He pinwheeled across the floor, driven by the force of the light and slammed against the back wall of the temple, his flames quenched by the frosted silver that froze his skin instantly. The crushing pain of ice spread through his veins and Perry screamed as the shock of it rippled through him.

Sir Douglas lay moaning in a tattered heap of smoking

rags, his arms a patchwork of oozing burned flesh with shards of bone visible beneath. Tendrils of shadow entwined with curls of smoke above him as the stench of charred skin filled the room.

Elf stepped through the open door, two huge muscled mutants behind her. She held one hand outstretched to hold Perry in place with the silver light, her eyes flashing an icy blue as she stalked toward her prey.

CHAPTER 20

As Elf walked in, Sienna looked at the floor, her eyes fixed on the thick wooden boards, noticing the whorls within even as she tried to dampen down the magic that flowed inside, trying desperately to stop the eddies of shadow emerging on her skin.

Elf had only glimpsed her briefly in the refugee camp that night. Perhaps she would not recognize her now? Smoke and shadow shrouded the room, and the young woman's gaze was fixed on Perry. But would like call to like?

Some part of Sienna wanted to stand and show the darkness on her skin, share the ties that bound them together and embrace the way the young woman so freely explored her magic. But if Elf realized the power that sat so close, Sienna knew she might not make it to the Tower of the Winds. Elf would take all she was and use it for her own ends.

Perry groaned and Elf stalked toward him, the others forgotten as she concentrated on her prey. She twisted her hand into a fist, crushing the silver light into a pinpoint. Perry doubled over, hands clutched to his belly where the beam focused.

She opened her fist again, her fingers spreading like a flower. The brilliance expanded, licking across Perry's skin as his flame awakened once more.

But this time, it was not under his control.

Elf tore it from him as she pulled the magic out, her breath rapid, her face transfigured into something like ecstasy as she fed on his power.

Perry cried out, his tortured body shuddering as he convulsed in pain.

Sir Douglas raised himself up onto one elbow, weakened by the attack but not finished yet. His face was human now, less shadow, more burned flesh. One piercing blue eye remained while the other was swollen shut, the eyelid red and oozing.

"Leave him." His voice trembled, but Sienna heard the edge of steel in his tone.

Elf tightened her grip. "So, this is your son. The one who chose his Mapwalker friends over you."

She tugged harder on the silver cord and Perry jerked once, then collapsed into spasm, his body sagging in on itself as energy was sucked from him.

Sienna wept as she watched her friend suffer, with no way to stop his end as she could not have stopped Elf killing Xander and his lion, Asada. In that moment, she wished for a different type of magic, one that would enable her to fight back. She wished for Mila's water, for Perry's fire, for Zoe's ability to manipulate the strings of the world, for anything but her own blood. She could escape right now, mapwalk out of here, but that would leave her friends behind. And she was nothing without them.

Elf laughed as she tore into Perry with both hands, teeth bared, nails ripping into the air, as her silver light dug deep within his bones for the last vestiges of power. He was silent now, a husk of the man he had been, his face pallid, eyes closed. Sienna felt the beat of his magic slow.

He was almost finished.

"Enough." Sir Douglas reached out one blackened, twisted hand. A bolt of flame shot from his outstretched fingers, cutting off Elf's silver blade of light and blocking its path. Perry's body slumped to the floor, his chest rising and falling in a jerky manner. He still lived, but not for much longer.

Elf turned, her expression alive with cold anger but Sienna saw something else there. Excitement for a confrontation she had clearly wanted for too long.

Sir Douglas had reined the young woman in, his power too much for her to challenge. But now the old man lay crumpled on the floor, the shadows that normally writhed about him in powerful arcs were now merely shreds.

"Leave him. He's mine to finish." Sir Douglas stared at Elf, his one good eye meeting her piercing gaze.

She smiled and shook her head. "Not anymore."

Elf raised her hands and shot darts of white light toward Sir Douglas.

He thrust out one palm, flames erupting around it, pushing back the white light, burning it with his crimson blaze. The hiss of steam erupted into the air as fire met ice. Elf reared back as the force hit her, but then she leaned into the fight, redoubling her efforts. She seemed to grow taller in stature as she called forth her powerful magic.

The last remaining shreds of shadow shrank from Sir Douglas, curling away from him like snakes deserting a home that would soon burn them alive.

Elf's silver shard of light inched its way closer, forcing him back. Sienna watched as the last shadows left his body, his face contorted in pain as he became more like the man who had come to her in the map shop that first day. It seemed a lifetime away now.

Elf smiled in triumph. She walked across the still burning timbers of the floor, raising her hands higher. As her light broke through his wall of flame, Sir Douglas gasped in agony.

She tightened her grip and tore the last vestiges of magic

from him. "Your time is over, old man. The Shadow favors me now."

He convulsed as coils of magic shuddered from him. Elf threw back her head and screamed in pleasure as she drank in his power.

A sudden explosion rocked the building, a series of blasts from outside at the vats. A heavy beam jolted loose above.

Elf looked up, her eyes widening as it dropped.

* * *

Mila heard the explosions from inside the church, a series of deep booms that rippled through the water. A moment later, the attack on the door stopped and the giant eels darted away back to the shore. She didn't know what had happened, but she could imagine the chaos of the drunken revelers on the beach running for the water. Food for the eels, after all.

She urged the children to their feet. "Quick, we need to get out of here while they're distracted."

Dawn shrank back on the bench. "I don't want to go out there."

Mila hunkered down in front of her. "They're gone, but not for long. We can swim to the opposite side, get out the water there. I can take you to a safe place."

Dawn looked up at Daniel. After a moment, the boy nodded.

They swam to the opposite side of the sunken church and Mila peered out the little window into the murky water. There could be more creatures waiting, but they had no time to wait and see.

She held her hands out, and the children took them, trusting her. Their skin reminded her of Ekon, a dissolving of flesh to water, something only their kind could do. She had to take these children home.

They darted together out into the gloom. None of them looked back.

* * *

As the beam fell, Elf jerked her arms up, shielding herself with magic and pushing the heavy beam toward Sir Douglas. The weight of the wood crushed him to the floor, pinning what remained of his body under the smoldering shaft. Burning embers tumbled down around them as the flames took hold.

Two more booms shook the building.

Screams from the panicked crowd outside.

Another beam came loose and crashed down. It glanced off Elf's shoulder, sending her to the ground with a cry. The mutant bodyguards surged forward. One enormous brute picked the young woman up in his arms, shielding her as they ran from the building even as the beams tumbled down behind them.

Zoe's chair tipped over in the blast and Sienna dived to stop her head hitting the floor. She wrapped her arms around her friend; her face only inches from where Sir Douglas lay unmoving, half-crushed beneath the fallen beam. His remaining eyelid flickered, and he breathed in shallow gasps, his lungs clearly constricted by the weight.

Perry sprawled only meters away, his body broken, his magic siphoned away, his mind possibly damaged beyond repair.

The shouts of a frantic crowd came from outside through the roar of the flames that licked at the beams. The shifting sound of wood collapsing. It wouldn't be long until they were buried in here or burned alive.

But there was one way out.

"Perry!" Sienna shouted, weeping as she called for her friend. "Can you hear me?"

If she could get to him, she could mapwalk them all out of here.

The sound of running footsteps and the creak of wood.

Two figures entered the disintegrating building, big men with weapons at their sides, faces obscured by the smoke. Sienna ducked quickly back behind the burning beam, desperately hoping they wouldn't see her.

"Sienna?"

His voice was everything she had longed for. Sienna looked out under the beam and her heart leapt at seeing the regal profile silhouetted against the flames.

"Finn. Finn, I'm here."

He turned at her voice. Their eyes met, and the world melted away. For a second, Sienna could believe that everything would work out, that he would save her and they would escape this terrible place and be together.

Then the building shifted once more, flames crackled and another beam fractured above her head.

Finn and his companion darted forward, shouldering through the burning wood, sheltering Sienna as they untied Zoe from the chair.

"Titus, carry her outside. I'll be right behind you."

Titus nodded, hoisting Zoe into his arms and barreling back out into the chaos beyond.

Finn put his arms around Sienna, pulling her close to his chest, his hands tender on her skin.

He looked down at Sir Douglas. "What about him?"

Sienna shook her head. "Perry first, he's over there. He's hurt."

Together, they climbed over the beams and dug through the fallen wood. Perry lay on his back, his face pale and waxy, ash in his hair, soot smeared over his skin. His eyes fluttered open as they helped him up to a sitting position.

"My father?" His voice rasped from flame-cracked lips.

Sienna pointed to the fallen beam. "He's pinned. Elf took his magic and if he's not dead already, he will be soon."

Perry tried to get up, but his legs crumpled beneath him.

Finn took his weight. "We have to get out of here. The building could collapse at any minute."

"Please. I need to see him."

Sienna could see the conflict in Finn's expression, his jawline taut with tension. The rebel leader had faced his own father on a battlefield, a man who still held the power of life and death over him.

Finn nodded, swiftly lifting Perry to his feet and helping him around the back of the beam to where his father lay.

Sir Douglas looked dead, a crushed corpse, but as Perry knelt and rested a hand on his blackened brow, the man opened his one good eye.

His lips parted in a sigh. "Son," he whispered.

Perry leaned closer, tears spilling down his cheeks. "I'm so sorry, Dad."

Sir Douglas closed his eye a moment and then opened it again. "Inside my cloak. Reach in."

Perry frowned and bent to his father's chest, easing his hand inside the burned clothing. He couldn't help but touch the weeping, blistered flesh, coating his fingers in sticky blood. But Sir Douglas was beyond feeling anymore and Perry thrust his hand in further. A second later, he withdrew his hand and uncurled his bloody fingers.

Sienna gasped at the sight of her grandfather's silver compass. Stolen by the man who had murdered him one stormy night in Bath in the grove of sacred plane trees in the center of the Druid's circle.

Sir Douglas looked up at Sienna. "Use it once more," he whispered, his voice slowing. "For Galileo."

His eye drooped shut as he let out a final breath. His head lolled to one side and Perry let out a sob.

A beam cracked overhead, and the sound of trampling footsteps came from outside.

"We're out of time." Finn grabbed Perry with one arm,

pulling him to his feet while he helped Sienna with the other.

The floorboards creaked underfoot, weakening even as they darted between falling beams. Burning embers and ash rained down as smoke filled the building with choking fumes. Sienna could barely see what direction they should go in, but Finn dragged them on.

A light ahead. The back door gaped open, the staircase burning up from below.

"Jump!" Finn shouted, half-dragging Perry over the edge. Sienna followed close behind, rolling as she hit the hard ground behind the scorching temple.

The crackling sound of flames filled the air alongside the screams and shouts of the panicked crowd. They flowed like a river away from the plaza, back to the barracks and shacks at the edges of the camp. Sienna pushed herself up quickly as two men ran past, unheeding of her on the ground. Another inch closer and they would have trampled her.

She stood up and turned to find Finn helping Perry, and Titus waiting with Zoe over his shoulder in a fireman's carry. Sienna wanted to be the one in Finn's arms, but Perry's face was blanched with grief and the aftermath of whatever Elf had done to him. She didn't know whether he still had any magic left, but they couldn't wait to find out.

"This way," Titus shouted and headed away up the hill, joining the throng.

Finn nodded at Sienna. "I'll help Perry. Go. I'll be right behind you."

Whatever was unsaid between them could wait. She turned and jogged after Titus, merging with the crowd and ducking down as they passed the mutant guards. But the sentries were distracted and waved everyone on, eyes fixed on the burning temple and the ruins of the plaza beyond.

At the top of the hill, Sienna turned to see what had them so mesmerized. The waters ran red at the edge of the lake, bodies torn apart by the giant eels that writhed in the shallows, razor-sharp teeth slashing soft flesh in a feeding frenzy. The explosions must have driven some of the crowd into the water, only to be met by the monsters that lurked just below the surface.

Sienna stifled a sob as she thought of Mila down there with the children. "Please make it back," she whispered, then turned and ran once more.

She caught up with Titus on the edge of the shantytown as he easily carried Zoe's slight frame over his broad shoulders. He turned to greet her, and she noticed the stain of blue on his fingertips.

He noticed her look and raised an eyebrow. "I'm a chemist."

She smiled. "Useful skill. Was that—?"

Titus nodded. "Our explosions. Yes. We came to the camp to destroy the manufacture of the drug these bastards peddle in the trader towns, but then Finn saw your friend dive into the lake. He can recognize an Earthsider from a mile away and had an inkling you might be close by." Titus hesitated for a moment, then sighed. "To be honest, I haven't seen him this alive for so long."

Warmth spread through Sienna at his words. Finn had missed her just as much as she had longed for him and that gave her hope.

Zoe stirred. Titus gently lifted her off his shoulders and set her down on the ground. She rubbed her eyes, blinking as she took in her surroundings. "What happened?"

Sienna knelt next to her. "It's okay. You're safe now."

Zoe reached up and grasped her hand, eyes wide in desperation. "Elf. We have to stop her. She's found a way to drain and concentrate magical power."

"I know," Sienna said softly. "That's how she killed Xander. She almost killed Perry back there and who knows how many others."

Titus frowned. "She must be the one responsible for adding the mutation magic to the Liberation."

Zoe nodded. "Yes, but it's much more than that. I heard her telling the old man, Sir Douglas, how she could use the shadow portal in the Tower of the Winds to reach all the Borderlands at once. How she could somehow bleed power from everywhere, then use it to finally blow apart the border and retake Earthside. I saw the look on his face, Sienna. He was scared. It must be possible. We have to stop her."

CHAPTER 21

TOGETHER, THEY MADE THEIR way back to the cave. Titus helped Zoe and Sienna over the wall into the rubbish heap beyond and Finn half-carried Perry, who grew weaker with every passing minute.

No one tried to stop them. No one even paid any attention as they climbed away from the mutant camp into the sanctuary of the cave system.

As they approached, Sienna kept looking up at the opening, hoping that Mila might have already arrived. But there was no sign of the Waterwalker, and when they made it inside, Mila had not returned.

Finn helped Perry to rest against the back wall and Zoe curled up next to him, both exhausted. Titus pulled food from his pack and shared it out with water from his canteen.

Sienna sat at the lip of the cave entrance and scanned the hill below for any sign of Mila or approaching danger from the camp. Finn came to sit beside her and she leaned into his warmth.

"I'm so glad you're here," she whispered.

He put his arm around her and pulled her close, kissing her hair. "I'm sorry I didn't make it earlier. You should have told me you were coming."

Sienna closed her eyes, and they breathed the night air together. Whatever anger and misunderstanding had passed between them mattered little now. There was only the moment and in this crack of time, Sienna belonged to Finn alone.

She raised her head and looked up into his dark eyes, stroked his cheek. He leaned down and in their kiss lay the promise of possibility, the hope that Borderlander and Earthsider could live in peace. A world where the moon rose on all kinds alike.

Sienna wanted to stay in that moment forever, lost in his soft mouth, but the sound of scraping on stone came from below, then the tumble of loose rocks on scree.

They broke apart and looked over the lip of the cave.

Mila scrambled up the incline, two children behind her.

Sienna wanted to shout in excitement, but the sound would echo in the valley and might alert the guards. She restrained her happiness by kissing Finn once more, her smile reflected in his glad expression. The team was wounded, but they were not finished yet.

Mila soon made it to the lip of the cave. She hugged Sienna and Finn, but the children hung back, their faces curious but shy.

"It's okay." Mila beckoned them forward. "These are my friends. You're safe now."

She introduced them, and the children solemnly nodded in greeting.

Titus pulled out some more food, and the children were soon chattering away happily with the big chemist. Finn went to join them, leaving Mila and Sienna to talk.

They sat at the cave entrance under the light of the moon, the camp below them calm now as the night wore on, intoxicated revelers sleeping off the carnival and the stress of the day, blood and chaos chasing them through nightmares.

"I thought you might not make it back," Sienna said, taking her friend's hand. "I saw what those creatures did to bodies on the shoreline."

Mila squeezed her hand with a rueful smile. "It was pretty crazy down there." She shook her head. "I just had to go after them … And it's more than that." She paused, a moment of silence before a sigh of acceptance. "I need to take the children to Ganvié and to be honest, I want to go home. To my true home, that is."

Sienna heard the longing in Mila's voice and wished she could feel that certain about where she belonged.

Mila continued. "I felt something rare under the lake. An elemental joy that has always been out of reach on Earthside. I can't leave that behind again. I can't go back to living outside my true nature."

Sienna smiled. "I know that leaving Ekon was difficult for you. I saw how you transformed when you were with him."

"I think more of my kind still exist under the waves, but they've become one with the water somehow. Perhaps I can find them with Ekon and the twins by my side — after we finish this mission, of course. I'll come with you to the Tower of the Winds first. We'll finish this together."

Sienna sat silent for a moment. She thought of the woman in the mosaic on the cave wall under the impossible mountain. She had been alone — and perhaps that was the only way. Perry and Zoe were injured. Finn and Titus had no magic. Mila would be the only one who could stand with her — but the path ahead was dangerous and Sienna knew she had to face whatever it was alone. If Mila came to the Tower of the Winds, she might not make it out again. She had a chance for happiness, for a life fulfilled, and Sienna wanted that for her friend. Her own future was uncertain, but Mila and the twins could start anew.

"I don't want you to come," Sienna said, pushing down the tears that threatened. "I don't need you, anyway."

Mila frowned. "What do you mean? I can fight by your side. We're a team."

"Not anymore." Sienna looked into Mila's eyes. "I don't

want you to bring the children and they need you more than I do. We'll be fine, Mila, really. I want you to go to Ganvié. If we need you, I'll send word somehow."

"If you're sure."

"I am." Sienna put every ounce of confidence into her words, knowing that Mila would follow if she did not dissuade her.

"Then I'll go to Ganvié tomorrow." Mila turned to look back into the cave. The others were too far away to hear them. She leaned in close. "But be careful, Sienna. I know something calls you from the Tower of the Winds. I know the marks on your skin have spread."

Sienna flushed. "Is it obvious?"

"Not to everyone, but you and I … well, we've discovered a lot on these last missions. I've seen you change to become a powerful Blood Mapwalker. Your destiny draws you on, as does mine."

"But not together anymore," Sienna whispered as she leaned in and they hugged, clinging to each other for a moment, then they parted.

"I left Zippy with a friend who loves him," Mila said. "And a letter for Bridget in the canal boat explaining everything, but I won't go back this time. I am not of Earthside anymore. Perhaps I never really was."

Sienna hugged her friend again, hiding her tears against Mila's hair, smelling the fresh water of the lake on her skin. They sat for a moment, holding each other tight, both aware of an ending they hadn't expected to experience so soon.

Sienna pulled away and wiped her eyes. "How will you get to Ganvié?"

Mila shrugged. "The watercourses will guide us. We'll travel up river and find our way from there. I'm drawn back somehow, like a compass needle pointing true north." She looked out at the horizon. "I know Ekon will welcome us."

"He will." Sienna rose to her feet. "But I hate goodbyes so this is temporary. I'll come visit when I can."

Mila smiled and stood up to join her. "Of course." She gave a cheeky grin. "And bring Finn with you."

Sienna looked back into the cave where Finn sat by the fire, the light dancing off his angular cheekbones as he played a dice game with the children. They laughed, leaning on his legs, trusting him instinctively. With their dark skin, they could be his and Sienna was suddenly struck with a glimpse into a possible future.

Finn looked up at her, a question in his eyes.

She smiled and went to join him. They all needed to rest before the day to come.

* * *

The rays of dawn reached into the cave and touched Sienna's cheek. She opened her eyes to see coral light bathing the sleeping group, as if blessed by some heavenly benediction. She nestled back into Finn's embrace, trying to fix the moment in her mind.

Sienna thought of her father and Bridget back on Earthside, the same dawn rising over the Ministry. Mapwalking had broken their love apart, taken everything from them both. Her father was a crippled husk, his body and mind shattered by that final mission. Bridget had given her very blood to the service of the Ministry, trapped in the guise of the Illuminated for who knows how many generations. Her grandfather's skin lay in the Blood Gallery, his life sacrificed for a portal he couldn't even ultimately defend. Sienna pulled his compass from her pocket.

The silver gleamed in the morning light and she opened the case to reveal the five-pointed compass rose and the city of Bath etched in tiny lines within. The abbey, the map shop, the Circus, the river, the canal. Five places to anchor her back to Earthside.

Sienna clutched the compass tightly in her hand. If the border had been open, she could cut herself right now, map-walk through the power of her blood and take Perry and Zoe home. But she would have to leave Finn behind once more — and besides, the border was still closed, and her fight was here now.

Zoe's words about Elf ran through her mind. What did the young woman intend at the Tower of the Winds?

There was only one way to find out. It was time she faced whatever called in her nightmares.

"Morning," Finn whispered, his breath caressing her ear as he shifted position, wrapping his arms more tightly about her. As he pulled her closer. Sienna could feel his muscular body down the length of her back and she longed to stay right there, sheltered in his warmth. But the sun rose higher in the sky and every minute that passed was another minute that Elf traveled before them.

Titus sat up, yawned and stretched his arms. He looked over and smiled as he caught Sienna's gaze. "I'll make coffee. You lovebirds stay right there."

He set up a small fire near the entrance to the cave then pulled his pack over, scouring through it for matches.

"Damn, I must have dropped them when we set off the charges." He looked over at Finn. "You have any?"

"Let me do it." Perry's voice was weak but Sienna heard determination as he rocked up to his hands and knees and crawled to the pile of wood, Zoe helping him with a steady arm. Sienna sat up, Finn sitting with her, all of them willing him on.

Perry reached the pile of kindling as the rising sun caught his face with an orange glow, brightening his pale countenance. He reached a hand out, extended his fingers, looked down into his palm. His brow furrowed as he concentrated, curling and tensing his grip until his hand was almost a claw.

Sienna held her breath, willing him to find that spark, desperate to know what was left of his power.

CHAPTER 22

THE SECONDS TICKED PAST with not even a flicker.

Perry tightened his fist and slammed it down on the cave floor. He hung his head and then looked out to the horizon, biting his lip in frustration. Zoe wrapped her arms around his shoulders, silent in her support.

Sienna wondered whether his power was gone completely or just weakened. In such a state, should she really take him with her to the Tower of the Winds? With Mila leaving, she needed Perry — but he could be more of a liability in this state.

Finn rummaged in his bag and pulled out a box of matches. He tossed them to Titus, who lit the fire and soon had water boiling for coffee.

"What did I miss?" Mila sat up, her expression confused at the tense silence in the cave.

"Nothing," Perry whispered, a hint of bitterness in his tone. "Nothing at all."

The twins stirred, their small hands reaching for Mila as they awoke. Sienna smiled to see the way her friend gathered them to her, a Waterwalker family on its way home. At least something good had come out of the camp.

Titus made coffee, a thick brew in the Turkish style, a shot of caffeine to send them off suitably fired up. Sienna sipped at hers, trying to hold off the inevitable. But as the sun rose higher over the lip of the cave, she knew they had to go.

There were clouds on the horizon, a gathering storm that would sweep over the camp within hours. Mila could leave in the shelter of its rainfall and the rest of them would be long gone by then.

"Pack up," she said. "We need to leave."

It didn't take long to ready themselves, but it took longer for Mila to say goodbye to everyone. Perry clung to her the longest and Sienna had to turn away to hide the tears in her eyes. She had to believe that the team would be together again — sometime, somewhere.

She put her hands on the wall of the cave, cold stone anchoring her to this place in this moment. Once she took the team through the blood map, her path was set, but she could see no other way forward.

The border must open once more or Earthside would be wracked by increasing natural disaster. But the opening must be controlled otherwise the Borderlanders would stream over and take what they believed to be theirs. If Elf was truly going after whatever lay in the Tower of the Winds, Sienna had to get there first.

They had one advantage. Elf had to travel by road, and even with her mutant pack running at full pace, she would still be hours away. The rest had been worth it. Sleep in Finn's arms had renewed Sienna's strength and revived her sense of purpose. She was ready.

She drew on the stone wall with a fingertip, lightly etching a map over the rock. One that seemed carved on her heart. She had seen it so many times in her nightmares. It would be easy to travel there. All she had to do was follow the voice that called and drop down through the clouds to the tower. She could find the place easily. The only question was what waited there — and whether she could resist the pull of the Shadow once inside.

"Sienna?" Mila touched her arm gently.

Sienna turned to embrace her friend. "Go safe."

Mila nodded, her eyes betraying both her sadness but also excitement at the start of a new adventure. "One time of life ends, another begins."

Sienna smiled. "Perhaps for both of us."

Mila stood back by the cave entrance, the twins on either side, hands curled in hers, their faces curious but trusting. They had seen so much of magic, but perhaps never the strange exit of a Blood Mapwalker.

Sienna turned her back to them so they would not see her pull out the ritual knife, the sharp blade almost a friend to her now. She cut into the side of her palm, blood welling fast, and used it to sketch over the lines on the wall.

Her fingers moved with accuracy and speed, as if the map was carved inside her, just waiting to burst free. Sienna's skin itched, and she sensed the dark whorls eddy and throb as they drew closer to their home.

As she inscribed the last line, she reached out her other hand. Perry and Zoe, Finn and Titus grasped it, palm over palm, holding onto each other as Sienna drew them into the map. As the world shifted, she met Mila's gaze in one final goodbye.

The caves fell away. Below them, the expanse of the camp and beyond that, the lake of strange creatures, then the river heading off toward the coast where Mila would swim home. Sienna rose higher, reveling in the sensation of freedom as she reached out across the Borderlands with her magic.

She flew like one of the giant eagles they encountered in the eyrie back in the search for the Map of Plagues, with keen eyesight that could pick out detail in the expanse below. Beyond the towering sharp peaks, a track stretched out into an arid plain spiked with cactus and patches of scrub. A dust cloud headed east, thrown up by the running feet of a pack of mutants. Elf was amongst them, carried on the back of one beast and beyond, in the distance, the Tower of the Winds.

Sienna circled up into the clouds that obscured the sun. Without the distraction of the world below she could hear her name more clearly, a whisper that rippled down her spine, causing her to ache for some dark pleasure she could not quite name.

Sienna.

Did Elf hear her name called like this? Were they both summoned for the final reckoning? Sienna shivered as the clouds darkened and a sudden rainstorm blew across the sky, bringing with it rolls of thunder.

A flash of lightning caught a jagged outline above, the wings of a huge beast with talons raised like a hunter. She had seen something like it when imprisoned within the shadow weave, and she had no wish to encounter such a creature again.

Sienna dived back down through the clouds, emerging close to the Tower of the Winds. The fortress spiraled into the sky, a citadel of many levels. It was made from pieces of black stone locked together in intricate patterns with fragments of obsidian and black onyx mixed in with the pocked surface of volcanic lava and glossy agate. Polished to a sheen, the tower rose with curves as smooth as glass, impossible to climb from the outside even if someone were to brave its heights.

She soared around it, sensing the intensity of shadow in the highest part of the tower. Some part of her wanted to land right there, cast the others off into the space between the worlds and go alone to meet whatever waited. Her blood hammered through her veins, a pulse that demanded to be shed. For what was a Blood Mapwalker unless her power could be wielded?

Sienna.

The whisper grew louder now with the heady sensuality

of a lover's call. It promised gifts and pleasure, and the dark whorls of shadow on her skin wanted only to give in.

But the weight of her friends anchored her, and Sienna fought against the desire to rush to the summit. She swooped lower, spotting a library through arched windows with giant books chained to wooden lecterns and shelves full of ancient tomes. She plunged down in her mind's eye and when she could feel the solid floor under her feet and smell the faint musty vanilla scent of old books, Sienna opened her eyes.

The others lay on the floor around her. Titus coughed and retched, reeling from his first mapwalking experience. The others were more used to the nausea and lay still for a moment as they recovered. Sienna gazed down at them. They were weak, pitifully so.

The sudden thought was shocking. These were her friends. How could she think that way?

Finn sat up and looked at her, his eyes widening as he mouthed a prayer to the goddess. Sienna saw fear in his expression where such a short time ago, there had been only love. What was happening?

She gazed down at her bare arms, now deeply mottled with black symbols that writhed on her skin as if alive with dark magic. There was a mirror against one bookcase and she walked to it quickly. The same marks now covered her face and neck, signs of shadow whirling on her skin, winding in and out of her tattoos depicting the city of Bath. Sienna's entire body was now a fusion of light and dark, a battleground for the Shadow — and it felt good.

Sienna knew that Finn was right to be afraid. Her power was rising. She needed to ascend the tower but the others must not come with her. She didn't want them to see what she might become — or what she might do to them once she reached her goal.

* * *

Zoe rolled onto her hands and knees and pushed down the queasy sensation in her stomach. They should have a name for the travel sickness that came with mapwalking, but then naming it would only make it seem more normal, and there was nothing normal about traveling through a map made from the blood of a friend. She looked around for Perry, saw him lying near her, his face pale, no longer traveling with ease. She reached out a hand—

A gasp.

Zoe looked up to see Finn's horrified expression as Sienna gazed at herself in a mirror. Dark whorls of shadow eddied across her skin and in the reflection, Zoe saw Sienna transformed. The blood that ran through her veins now channeled the power of the Shadow and yet, her eyes were still clear and bright. Somehow, she managed to keep the darkness in some kind of balance — but for how long?

Zoe's vision shifted, and she saw the strings of the world bend around Sienna, warping away from her as if repelled by her aberration, then attracted back in. They hummed with increased power, charged by her very presence. Whatever was happening, it intensified the closer Sienna came to the peak of the tower.

It wasn't much further now, but this was a strange place to make their last stand. The vast library was round with a central staircase the only route up from below. A single narrow doorway with stairs of black stone wound up to the higher levels.

Mahogany bookshelves spread like spokes from the middle of the room, leading to arched windows at the end of each corridor, allowing light to illuminate the halls of knowledge within. There were books here that were rare on Earthside, heresies thought lost to history, but each found a place off the edge of the map. Vanished ideas melded into something new, every dark entreaty giving power to the Shadow. Some of the books had crumbled in place, their spines damaged by the years. In another time, Zoe would have taken them for restoration and granted the tomes a new life. But not today.

"They're almost here," Titus shouted, pointing out the window at a dust cloud approaching. Zoe could just make out figures on the wide open plain. A pack of mutants ran on thick limbs, Elf riding high on the shoulders of one colossal beast.

"They'll have to come this way to get up to the top." Finn leaned over the balustrade of the spiral staircase to look down to the levels below. "We need to block this as much as we can." He glanced over at Sienna. "We'll buy you time for whatever you need to do up there."

She nodded and without a second look, walked through the narrow doorway to ascend the black stone stairs.

Finn watched her go. As soon as she disappeared, his expression hardened. He dragged one of the huge lecterns toward the hole and put his back against it, muscles bulging, legs straining with the effort. Titus joined him and with a crash, the lectern fell down onto the intricate staircase.

It was a start, but they would need much more to stop anyone coming up.

Zoe dragged herself to her feet, pushing aside the leaden weight in her limbs as she helped Perry up. Together they all pulled piles of books off then shouldered the heavy shelves onto one side, sliding them over the holes left in the staircase, slowly forming a great pile of heavy wood blocking the only entrance.

A dull thud came from way below. The sound of a massive door opening.

"Keep going." Finn's chest heaved in great breaths as he pushed another bookcase onto the pile, now stacked three deep.

Heavy footsteps came from below, shouts in a guttural tongue and the high-pitched voice of Elf urging the mutants on.

A hammering sound thumped through the library. The bookcases shook, jolting up and down as if the heavy wood were nothing more than kindling.

Finn and Titus drew their swords, stepped back into a fighting stance as they faced the stairwell, bodies taut as the warriors took their last stand.

Perry retreated to one arched window, his back against the wall as he raised his hands, palms up. He closed his eyes and whispered something, a prayer or an entreaty, it didn't matter which. Zoe could see the frustration on his face as he desperately searched within himself for a tiny glimmer of the flame he once called easily to his bidding. But his palms remained empty. Not even a flicker of light left. She wanted to go to him, but Zoe knew she could offer nothing that would help. He had to face this moment alone.

The thumping came again.

The sound of cracking wood and splintering timber. The middle set of bookshelves crashed down, opening a hole big enough to climb through.

Two mutants surged up through the gap, faces contorted with rage. They looked similar to the giant Hashim, but where he had carried Zoe with gentle arms, these beasts now swung clenched fists like steel hammers.

One forced Finn back with a flurry of blows, oblivious to the cuts and slashes that the rebel Borderlander managed to land.

Titus went down under the blade of another, a deep gash on his forehead, his arms and torso quickly bloody and bruised. Finn rushed to stand over the body of his friend, sword flashing in the air, faster than ever, a warrior in his prime.

More mutants clambered out of the hole, hacking with their short swords. Finn parried and thrust, dancing around the lumbering creatures.

But they kept pouring from the hole. There were too many. They were almost out of time.

Perry tried desperately to rekindle his flame in the maelstrom of the library, but Zoe could see he was broken.

She stepped in front of him and shifted her vision. The weave of the world appeared in shades of gold and silver thread shot through with black. But now she understood that the Shadow was just one aspect of the whole and it could be manipulated just as other threads.

Zoe reached out and weaved the cords together, creating a net around the mutants. With one tug, she pulled them away from Finn.

They struggled and grunted, striking at the air as they tumbled over one another, clutching at nothing. The net was invisible but as strong as her magic, and Zoe clenched her fists as she entangled them further.

Finn fell to his knees, gasping for breath in a moment of welcome respite. Perhaps they could hold off the attack after all.

A sudden white light shot out of the well of the staircase, blowing the Mapwalker team backward and tearing the strings of the magic net apart.

The mutants rolled out of their entanglement, bellowing with rage.

Elf rose out of the staircase behind them in a blaze of silver light. The jagged edge of a bolt of lightning with as much fury as the oncoming storm. She looked down upon them, cold violence in her gaze. She raised her hands for the slaughter.

CHAPTER 23

Sienna ran up the stairs toward the top of the tower. The sound of fighting below soon faded to nothing as she climbed higher. The staircase narrowed, winding tighter as she rose. The walls seemed to suck in the light from the tiny arrow-slit windows, smothering it with pitch like a dying animal sucked to the bottom of a peat bog.

Her footsteps slowed as she reached an open wooden door carved with runes of power.

Sienna.

The voice she had heard high in the clouds was now a caress, inviting her in.

Sienna pulled her grandfather's compass from her pocket, holding it in her hands like a talisman, anchoring her to Bath. Her home, her family, her world.

She stepped inside.

The circular room had high ceilings with thick wooden beams that met in the middle, vaulted like a cathedral. Between each, arched windows hung with heavy drapes that must look out over the plains in every direction. Etchings covered every surface of the walls, the stone carved into tableaux of war and violence, plague and suffering, lust and cruelty. The shadow side of humanity's existence.

Sienna tore her eyes away from the depravity and stepped

further into the room. Shadows shifted around the walls, snaking behind the drapes, pooling around the corners of the beams.

The metallic stink of dried blood hung heavy in the air, evidence of recent sacrifice to the dark power that ruled here. The remains of an offering lay on a stone altar against one wall, a dismembered corpse the size of a child. Sienna gripped the compass tighter, her skin crawling with the sense of being watched.

A circle lay marked out in the middle of the room, bounded by a ring of skulls. They were all different sizes, some animal, some human, others of mutant origin, some hideously disfigured, others from creatures long extinct on Earthside.

Within the ring, a vortex of black energy spiraled up toward the roof and high above, an opening led out to the sky. Inside the whirlwind, a dark figure spun in slow spirals, features obscured by tendrils of mist, its shape concealed by folds of midnight cloth that merged with the eddies of shadow.

Sienna.

The voice was all-consuming now, and a longing rose inside her, the marks on her skin calling like to like.

Sienna reached out a hand. The edge of the whirlwind licked along her skin, tendrils of black mist emerging as if to join with her flesh. For a second, there was tension, a skin on the tornado — then it broke, like the surface of water parting. It pulled her inside, the silver compass falling unheeded to the floor.

She gasped at the chill, the cold of the depths below ice caps, darkness tinged by blue light from a world now out of reach above. Creatures swam just out of sight with scything teeth ready to tear her apart, scuttling legs and unseeing eyes waiting to devour what remained. The sound of her pulse pounded through the water and below that, the howling of trapped souls drowned in the pitch black below.

Sienna reached out for the surface, desperately clawing her way up, but her limbs were too heavy, her lungs tight to bursting.

She wouldn't make it.

A lithe figure dived in from the ice above and reached for her hand, soft skin but with a powerful strength. As her vision narrowed, Sienna grasped hold and let herself be dragged back up to the world above.

As her head broke the surface, she took huge gasps of life-giving air. Her rescuer helped her to shore — not a world of ice, but a meadow of green grass, cherry trees and dappled light. Pink blossom blew on a warm summer breeze and flowers spiraled around her as she lay on the bank, the touch of soft petals on her cheeks.

Sienna.

Her rescuer was a young woman, her features perfectly sculpted like a Renaissance portrait. A robe of Marian blue clung to her body, wet from the water, and a silver mist hung around her like an aura. The woman from the mosaic at the heart of the border.

Her eyes were the shifting shades of opal and Sienna thought she could see a touch of Xander, maybe a hint of Sir Douglas. The silver hair at her temples mirrored an echo of Elf, yet the woman seemed ageless and Sienna could sense her deep wisdom. How long had she been here sustaining the Borderlands? There was so much Sienna wanted to know.

Let me show you.

The woman reached out a hand, and Sienna took it gladly. Together they spun into the air, up into the sky above the meadow and into the clouds away from the tower. They flew across the realm of the Borderlands, rich and teeming with life. So much to explore and learn about. A beautiful chaos, so different to the cornered world of Earthside where everything was ordered and limited. Sienna knew she could never be her complete self there. She could never use her magic in the way she was born to if she went back.

All this can be yours, Sienna. Join us and we will bring down the border. One world, together at last.

* * *

As Elf rose on a pillar of blinding silver light, anger surged through Perry in a burning white-hot heat. She had taken his father from him. She would not take Zoe and Sienna and his friends.

Perry let his grief ignite and in that moment, the spark caught within. He raised his hands, opening his palms as fireballs formed and caught alight in blazing crimson dancing with flecks of electric blue. He tapped into the last of what remained of his magic, conjuring the words his father had spoken as he died. *For Galileo.*

Perry roared the cry of the phoenix who rises once more within the flame. His entire body flared into a blaze and he ran full-tilt across the library floor, fire catching the surrounding wood.

Elf turned in surprise and reached out in a blaze of light —

Perry leapt, spun in the air, and her beam glanced off his shoulder.

He slammed into her, a human pillar of flame. He wrapped his arms around her and as every cell of his body transformed into fire, Perry split open with metamorphosis, screaming in agony as he became more heat than skin, more flame than bone.

Within the ring of his grasp, Elf twisted and shuddered, her skin melting. He held her ever more tightly, burning through to the white of her bones, blood boiling, her hair on fire, eyes bulging as she screamed in torment.

Smoke rose around them, an offering to the ancient gods, those who had split the worlds apart so long ago. Perry felt

Elf sag in his arms and sensed her spirit burn up alongside their fused flesh.

With his last fiery breath, he spun into a pillar of flame, twisting down through the wooden staircase, burning a giant hole and pulling the last of the mutants down with him.

* * *

Zoe gasped for breath as the library burned. Smoke billowed out of the chasm in the center, embers dancing in the air like fireflies as ash rained down. The staircase had collapsed and only the roar of flames came from below. She clutched a hand to her mouth, tears streaming from her eyes, a sob erupting from her throat. Perry was truly gone.

In that last moment, she had witnessed his transformation from man to a creature of flame and burning wind, a fierce magic that ripped through his very flesh. He had become a master of his craft in those last moments — and it had cost him everything.

Zoe sat for a moment, her back against the stone of the tower. In the haze of smoke, it seemed as if she were here alone with the crackle of fire and the creak of burning wood. Was this really the end of the Mapwalker team at the top of the tower at the edge of the world? How could they have traveled so far and failed so badly?

But then she thought of Perry's face, his determination in those final moments. His sacrifice set a fire within Zoe's own soul. If he could summon so much in those last seconds, then she could, too.

She reached out and tested the strings of the world. Somehow, there was still balance. The Shadow had not won yet. Sienna was above in the tower and down here — she tested the cords — yes, Finn and Titus still lived.

Zoe pulled her sleeve down and held it over her mouth

and nose as she crawled through the wreckage of the library, coughing in the dense smoke. She sensed the heaviness of the men before she saw them. Broken bodies, unconscious from the pain of their wounds, barely breathing.

Finn lay face down over Titus, shielding his friend from the worst of the fire even as his own back lay scarred and ragged from mutant claws and embers from fallen beams.

Zoe grabbed Finn's arms and tugged him sideways off Titus's body and out along the corridor to the window. Muscles screaming, she dashed back through the smoke to do the same for Titus, laying him next to his friend.

Maybe the fresh air would revive them. Maybe together, they could help Sienna.

"Finn," Zoe croaked, her voice hoarse from the smoke. She stared down at the rebel leader's handsome face, sooty with ash and bloody from his wounds. "Wake up, please."

Finn stirred. His eyelids fluttered as he groaned and reached for Zoe's hand.

"Sienna," he gasped from his burned throat, his voice breaking with the effort. His face contorted with pain and Zoe could see how much it cost him to speak.

Zoe squeezed his hand. "It's okay. I'll go to her. Follow when you can."

She saw doubt in the rebel Borderlander's eyes, but Zoe knew he couldn't make it up those stairs right now, let alone face whatever lay in the tower above.

"It will be okay." She tried to hide the desperation in her voice. Finn and Titus were out of action, so she would have to go alone to face whatever was left in this dark place. Creatures of nightmare or Sienna herself, transformed.

Zoe left the men and crawled around the perimeter of the library, one hand on the rough wall to guide her. After a few meters, she turned back. Finn and Titus had already faded from view, obscured by the billowing smoke.

She was alone.

The black staircase emerged from the gloom. Zoe pulled herself to her feet and began to climb. She could hear something in the tower above, a cacophony of sound that drowned out the flames below. But she couldn't hear Sienna.

Zoe ran up the steps, driving herself on with every ounce of energy she had left. Was she already too late?

CHAPTER 24

Zoe reached the top of the stairs and rushed through the door, her breath ragged from running. Hideous figures carved on the walls around her seemed to move as she walked past, trapped in grotesque portraits of suffering, writhing in unending agony.

Smoke whirled in the air from the fire below, along with shadows that formed into tattered creatures of claw and fang. Zoe's heart hammered in fear, but she forced herself to step further into the room.

Sienna spun slowly in a vortex of shadow in the center of a circle of skulls. Her eyes were closed, but she smiled in delight as dusky mist contorted around her, bearing her up into the air like a celebratory offering. The patterns on her skin twisted in dizzy formation. The sound of many voices joined in a chorus. A harsh discord, like all the wrong notes played at once, and behind them, the fleshy sound of beating, whips hitting flesh, the thud of fists, the cries of the tortured.

The silver compass lay on the floor next to the skulls, its face sprung open to show the five-pointed design and the lines of Bath within.

Zoe bent to pick it up. One of the shadow creatures lunged at her, swiping with claws of rotted flesh, the stench of the grave rising up around them. Zoe rolled sideways, grabbing the compass as she did so, pulling it to her chest with one hand.

The specter leapt upon her back, its skeletal fingers freezing her flesh as it tried to wrest the compass away. It opened its maw and instead of rotting teeth; the thing had writhing maggots inside. They tumbled out over Zoe. She wriggled and screamed as the things burrowed into her skin, her breath coming in terrified gasps.

She threw up her hands and opened her eyes, allowing her vision to shift. The strings of the world appeared, and she saw that the ghoul of smoke was merely a creature of lies and deception, the maggots merely motes of dust on her skin. Zoe grasped the cords of shadow, her fingers darting through the air as she twisted the threads together, binding the creatures behind a lattice of their own substance. They moaned and twisted in desperation, clawing for her eyes, but the net held.

She crawled to the outside of the circle of skulls, clutching tightly to the compass. The dark well reached to the edge of the bony perimeter and something inside told her not to step into that vortex or she would be lost in the world between, trapped in the obsidian shards in the temple below the border.

"Sienna," she shouted, but the cacophony that whirled about her friend drowned her voice.

She held up the compass and called once more into the maelstrom. "For Galileo, Sienna. For your grandfather. For Earthside."

* * *

High above the clouds, Sienna heard someone call her name. A voice from home. Zoe.

The beautiful woman by her side tugged on her hand, distracting her. She pointed down at a giant creature below them just under the waves, scales like a dragon with a long neck and powerful jaws. It was terrifying and glorious all at once — and part of her domain if she would just become one with the Shadow. A promise of the world held out in exchange for what? Her blood, her life?

Zoë's voice came again. It was faint, but Sienna could just make out her words. *For Galileo.*

A flash of memory and the world darkened. Sienna saw her grandfather in the copse of plane trees in the Circus on a stormy night in Bath. A pack of wolves closed around him as he painted the sigil of the Illuminated on the earth with his blood, then gave his life to seal the border. Sir Douglas in the robes of a wolf reached down and took the compass, an offering to the darkness that ruled his life. But her grandfather had vanquished the Shadow that night and his blood called to her now.

Dr Rachel's voice came back to her from the clinic. *The Shadow is not always what it seems.*

Sienna looked over at the ageless young woman whose hand she held so tightly, then down at the Borderlands below. She could not be up here. There was no icy water, no drowning. She had stepped into the vortex — she must still be down there. This was all some kind of vision designed to distract her.

A howling rose up and the wind whipped them as lashes of rain descended. The woman gripped her hand more tightly, her eyes fixed on Sienna's, a triumphant smile on her lips. Was it too late?

They fell out of the sky, tumbling together through darkness and hail, the clash of lightning as if the gods raged about them.

But Sienna pushed it all aside and opened her eyes.

She spun within the vortex of shadow — and she held the

dried hand of a desiccated corpse made from mis-matched pieces of mangled cadavers, those lost to the Shadow over generations. A husk somehow sustained by dark blood magic.

Sienna desperately tried to thrust the hand away from her, but the shriveled flesh had fused to her own, their skin merging together. The symbols on her body spun ever faster as the silver mist crept up her arm, bringing with it flashes of memory.

A young woman in robes of Marian blue tied to an altar within a circle of skulls, surrounded by hooded figures. Mapwalkers from long ago — those of the Illuminated and those of the Shadow, joined in one moment to split the worlds. They slashed her skin and as her blood ran red; they bound her with a net of magic to this place — a vortex to hold the worlds in balance created by a Weaver.

The woman had held equilibrium in place for a time, but over generations, Earthside Mapwalkers withdrew, leaving the Borderlands to the Shadow. It had taken hold and slowly, slowly, turned the world toward darkness.

But it needed a host, and the withered corpse before her was finished.

As the silver mist receded from what was left, the body began to crumble, leaving only ash and dust in its wake. It was up to Sienna's elbow now and she knew that once it reached her heart, she would no longer be able to stop it.

A rush of wind from the opening high above in the vaulted ceiling. The storm was almost overhead. Lightning flashed from heavy clouds, creatures of winged terror flying within. If the Shadow could not take her alive, then Sienna knew it would destroy this tower and all within it. Her friends would die, the border would remain closed, perhaps forever, and Earthside would be wracked with disaster.

She thought of her father and her grandfather, how much they had given to uphold the secrets of the Mapwalkers

— and Bridget, tied to the maps themselves, her life blood pulsing with ink.

This path was her true heritage. She had been lost before the Ministry with no purpose, no direction. She had always longed for the world beyond the map — and now she stood at the heart of it. The young woman had held the worlds in balance for generations. Perhaps she could, too.

It was a chance to renew the worlds, save Earthside, and give the Borderlands a chance to thrive. It was everything she had wanted — for Finn, for Mila and Ekon, for those back on Earthside.

The Shadow was within her and on her skin in the writhing symbols and yet, a part of her still clung to Earthside, to her Mapwalker lineage. Her grandfather's blood had closed the border that night, perhaps her own would open it again. *Use the compass once more,* Sir Douglas had whispered in his dying words. *For Galileo.*

Tears spilled down her cheeks as Sienna desperately searched for a way she could make it work — but every path led her back to this place. There was no other way, but she would go on her own terms. The compass would be her anchor to Earthside.

The silver mist rose higher and cold crept over her skin. She was almost out of time.

Sienna turned to the edge of the vortex. Zoe stood on the lip of the circle of skulls, holding out the silver compass. Her lips moved, but the wind drowned her words.

Sienna remembered the moment in the winds as they descended into Egypt. Zoe had heard the voice that time. Perhaps she could hear through the wind now.

"I need your help."

At the words, Zoe stopped speaking and nodded.

"There's only one way to stop this. Throw the compass in and then bind me with cords of light and shadow."

Zoe shook her head, her eyes wide with horror.

"You must do it." Sienna nodded down at the rising mist. "If the Shadow takes me first, I may not be able to balance the worlds. But this way … it gives us more time, Zoe. Do this and then go back to Bridget. Search the annals for another way. But now, I choose this path."

The desiccated corpse began to split into fragments, chunks of it breaking off to dissolve into the spinning wind.

"Hurry! We're out of time."

Sienna took the ritual knife from her pocket, the blade that her grandfather had used to shed his blood and save Earthside once before. As the wind whipped around her, she drew it down her arm, blood rising and spinning away, droplets joining the vortex.

Screams echoed from within the Shadow as the last of the corpse split into dark beads, joining with Sienna's blood. Like calling to like.

"Now!" Sienna shouted. She saw Zoe throw the compass as the mist rose to encompass her.

She sensed the expanse of the world outside, a blossoming of power within, that could rise up and spread across both lands. Sienna wanted to tear it all apart, ravage every last inch and absorb the power of those who thought they could stand against the Shadow.

The silver compass tumbled into the whirlwind.

It hung in the air, opening to reveal the lines of Bath, carved by her grandfather's hand. With the last of her strength, Sienna reached out and hugged it to her chest.

"For Galileo," she whispered as lines of silver, blood and shadow formed a net around her.

* * *

Zoe wept as she weaved the threads of the world together, her fingers flashing through the air as she created a lattice of magic, a net to hold Sienna within the Tower of the Winds. Tears ran down her cheeks as she trapped her friend within the vortex, Sienna's slender frame now obscured by swirling blood and ash.

She could only hope that she had done the right thing, that somehow Bridget would know how to undo it all, to set Sienna free once more. But deep within, Zoe knew this was the only way.

Fate had bound a Weaver to their journey for this purpose — and now that purpose was fulfilled. The path of her own heritage and Sienna's bloodline had always been entwined. Zoe understood the truth of that now. For Weavers had always known the lines of the world were spun by fate. They were only instruments of destiny, and now Zoe could see that her own path had always been laid out this way.

She stitched the final element of Sienna's bloody prison and stepped back from the edge, her hands dropping to her sides.

"No!" Finn limped into the tower, his hand clutched to his side, his clothes covered in ash. "What have you done?"

He staggered over and pushed Zoe roughly aside, then lunged at the vortex for Sienna. His hand bounced off the perimeter, leaving his knuckles bloody and bruised as if he had punched a wall. He tried again and again, every blow coming back at him until he fell to his knees, broken and exhausted.

He looked up with tears in his eyes as Sienna spun unseeing behind her cage of silver and crimson.

Zoe knelt down beside him. "It was her choice," she whispered.

Finn shook his head. "There was never anyone else. Your people sent her here for this, even if she didn't know it."

Zoe remembered the woman in the mosaic beneath the border and the book in the library that first day with the hand-sketched figure in ash. Perhaps he was right. Perhaps

Bridget had known all along. But had there been any other way?

The storm calmed outside, the sound of thunder rolling away to nothing. Blue sky opened up in the skylight above and the sound of birdsong filled the air.

Zoe stood up and pulled back the heavy drapes from one window, letting the light inside. A sunbeam struck the whirling vortex that surrounded Sienna and the remains of ash within dissolved. It shone with ruby and golden light, reflecting into every part of the room.

The altar with its grisly sacrifice crumbled to dust, and the shadow creatures dissolved in the light. The carved abominations in the walls turned into patterns of flowers and fruit, an abundance of nature.

Zoe turned around in wonder, a smile dawning on her face. Somehow Sienna had shifted the balance of power and the Shadow was no longer the dominant force in the Borderlands.

She turned to Finn. "Help me open them all."

Together, they pulled open the other drapes, allowing light to stream into every corner. As the tower brimmed full, the light rolled out the windows once more, down the sides of the building and out onto the plains beyond. Flowers bloomed in its wake, the air filled with the scent of summer as the golden hue spread into the distance, illuminating the Borderlands for the first time in generations.

CHAPTER 25

FINN STARED OUT THE window, Zoe beside him, as the land below bloomed under the golden light. There was a buoyancy in the air where there had only been heaviness before, a sense of the world pivoting.

"This is more than just the renewal of the border," he said. "It's the restoration of the land itself. The Borderlands can thrive again without the dominance of the Shadow." He spun around to look at the vortex where Sienna spun within. "She has changed everything. The Resistance can take back Old Aleppo, purge my father's forces. It's a new beginning."

He walked back to the edge of the circle of skulls and reached out a hand, holding it only a millimeter from the spinning vortex. It was as close as he could get to Sienna through the veil when just this morning he had woken with her in his arms. The warmth of her body, the smell of her hair, how she had fitted so perfectly against him. It was how he hoped to wake every day for the rest of his life, but now …

Finn bit his lip as he tried to hold back the tears that threatened. She had chosen to leave him for the final time and the blood of a Mapwalker was now the hope of the Borderlands. He would honor her sacrifice and live on for the land they both loved — but now he would do it alone.

* * *

In the library under the Ministry back in Bath, Bridget sensed a sudden tension in the maps, the pulsing of ink beat more strongly within her veins. The rustling around her grew louder as cartography began to shift and re-form, as if the very fabric of the world had shifted.

She turned to the desk and pulled out the volume of Mapwalker annals. She opened it to a page marked with a scarlet silk thread. A figure sketched in ash on its ivory pages, her features suddenly clear.

Sienna, wrapped in a shroud of shadow and light in the midst of a whirling vortex of blood. Her life force would sustain the border and keep the Shadow at bay — at least for a time. The border was renewed and the natural disasters would soon end on Earthside as the world moved freely once more.

Tears ran down Bridget's cheeks as she reached out a fingertip and touched the face of the young woman trapped within the Tower of the Winds. Sienna was bound to her Mapwalker destiny just as Bridget was herself shackled to the library, a balance of Blood Cartographers until their lifespans ended or someone else took their place.

A gasp came from behind her, then a low moan of despair. Bridget turned to see John staring down at the sketch of his daughter. He sank to his knees and Bridget knelt to embrace him as they mourned the end of one time and the beginning of another.

* * *

Mila felt a shift in the water as she darted between the ripples of the river heading west toward the coast. It was as if all sharp edges became smooth for a moment and then reset themselves, like an earthquake passing beneath the mantle of the earth, lifting and lowering everything in its wake.

She glanced behind to check on the twins and by the look on their faces; they felt it too. Something had changed in the Borderlands and somehow, Mila knew that Sienna had made it to the Tower of the Winds.

They swam fast over submerged boulders, translucent skin flashing in the sunlight that dappled down through the water. Mila led the twins on. No time for stopping, and no need to. They all reveled in the freedom of being one with the water.

Up ahead, Mila heard the thundering of a waterfall. The river frothed, churning as it became shallow in places, and carving deep in others. Eddies and whirlpools formed at the sides. Daniel slipped into one, laughing with delight as he spun around. Dawn joined him, and the twins flew in circles hand in hand, dancing in the water.

Mila smiled as she watched them play, remembering her own solitary life in the canals of London and later in Bath. No one understood her. No one laughed with her. But that would all change now.

The Mapwalker team had been her home for a time, but losing Xander had been a heavy blow. Sienna would always be a friend, but her powerful blood meant she stood apart and her choices were beyond reach now.

Finn's words in the cave at Ganvié echoed back to her: *There are so few of your kind.* And yet, here they were, three lost Waterwalkers heading for home.

"Come on, you two," Mila called out. "I'll show you what fun really is."

She beckoned and then turned in the water, darting ahead of them through the rapids as they followed her with whoops of delight.

Mila dived down into the depths before the waterfall met the edge of the cliff and then leapt like a dolphin up out of the froth and into the air.

She spun around, her body diaphanous in the sunlight, a figure of water droplets and air, her laugh the tinkle of rain on stone. The twins leapt just behind her, shrieking with joy. The three of them plunged down the falls into the pool below and then on — toward Ekon and Ganvié.

THE END

ENJOYED MAP
OF THE IMPOSSIBLE?

Thanks for joining Sienna and the Mapwalker team in *Map of the Impossible*. If you enjoyed the book, a review would be much appreciated as it helps other readers discover the story.

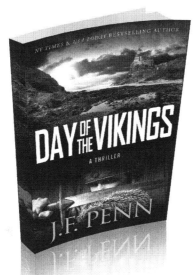

Get a free copy of the bestselling thriller, *Day of the Vikings*, an ARKANE thriller, when you sign up to join my Reader's Group. You'll also be notified of giveaways, new releases, and receive personal updates from behind the scenes of my books.

Click here to get started:

www.JFPenn.com/free

Day of the Vikings, an ARKANE thriller

A ritual murder on a remote island under the shifting skies of the aurora borealis.

A staff of power that can summon Ragnarok, the Viking apocalypse.

When Neo-Viking terrorists invade the British Museum in London to reclaim the staff of Skara Brae, ARKANE agent Dr. Morgan Sierra is trapped in the building along with hostages under mortal threat.

As the slaughter begins, Morgan works alongside psychic Blake Daniel to discern the past of the staff, dating back to islands invaded by the Vikings generations ago.

Can Morgan and Blake uncover the truth before Ragnarok is unleashed, consuming all in its wake?

Day of the Vikings is a fast-paced, supernatural thriller set in London and the islands of Orkney, Lindisfarne and Iona. Set in the present day, it resonates with the history and myth of the Vikings.

If you love an action-packed thriller,
you can get Day of the Vikings for free now:

WWW.JFPENN.COM/FREE

Day of the Vikings features Dr. Morgan Sierra from the ARKANE thrillers, and Blake Daniel from the London Crime Thrillers, but it is also a stand-alone novella that can be read and enjoyed separately.

AUTHOR'S NOTE

Thanks for reading *Map of the Impossible*. I hope you enjoyed the adventure. This is the end of the trilogy that encompasses Sienna's Mapwalker journey, but I have some ideas for Mila and Zoe, so you never know, there may be more Mapwalker adventures to come.

I always like to include an Author's Note in my novels as I love the research process as much as the creative part of writing. You can find images used in my research on my Pinterest board: www.pinterest.com/jfpenn/map-of-the-impossible

Inspiration for the story

The Map of the Impossible was inspired by the oldest map of the underworld found inside an ancient Egyptian coffin inscribed 4000 years ago. It was intended to help the dead pass through a series of challenges including snake charmers, high paths, and the watchers.

https://egyptfwd.org/Article/6/712/Oldest-Map-of-The-Underworld-Found-Inside-An-Ancient-Egyptian

The ibis room was inspired by pictures of mummified ibis and an article that mentioned 4 million sacred ibis mummies found in the catacombs of Tuna el-Gebel and 1.75 million discovered in the ancient burial ground of Saqqara as votive offerings to the god Thoth. The thought of millions of mummified ibis coming to life is pretty terrifying!

https://www.theguardian.com/science/2019/nov/13/experts-crack-mystery-ancient-egypt-sacred-bird-mummies

The antidote to belladonna is Physostigmine which is

found in the Calabar Bean and the manchineel tree.

The idea of Zoe's weaver magic was inspired by The Lady of Shalott poem by Alfred Lord Tennyson and the gorgeous painting by John William Waterhouse.

A note on strange times

I started the book in November 2019, so the idea of natural disaster impacting the world while the borders closed had nothing to do with the pandemic. But as it turned out, I wrote most of the story whilst in lockdown in Bath, UK, in the spring of 2020.

As I write this final note, we are still in the summer of coronavirus and while some borders are opening up, many remain closed, and I don't know when I will travel again. What a strange time in history, indeed.

ACKNOWLEDGMENTS

More than ever, a special thanks to my readers and my Pennfriends for continuing to support my books in what has turned out to be the wierdest year (2020 pandemic).

A special thanks to Michaelbrent Collings, whose positive encouragement (and terrific stories!) helped me through a difficult time.

Thanks to Mark McGuinness whose creative coaching helped me get through a lockdown process block and finish the book.

Thanks to my editor, Jen Blood, for continuing to understand my crazy brain, and to Wendy Janes for proofreading.

Thanks to Jane Dixon Smith at JDSmith-Design.com for the great cover design and print formatting.

MORE BOOKS BY J.F.PENN

Thanks for joining Sienna and the
Mapwalker team in *Map of the Impossible.*

Sign up at www.JFPenn.com/free to be
notified of the next book in the series and
receive my monthly updates and giveaways.

* * *

Mapwalker Dark Fantasy Thrillers

Map of Shadows #1
Map of Plagues #2
Map of the Impossible #3

If you enjoy **Action Adventure Thrillers**, check out the
ARKANE series as Morgan Sierra and Jake Timber solve
supernatural mysteries around the world.

Stone of Fire #1
Crypt of Bone #2
Ark of Blood #3
One Day In Budapest #4
Day of the Vikings #5
Gates of Hell #6
One Day in New York #7
Destroyer of Worlds #8
End of Days #9
Valley of Dry Bones #10
Tree of Life #11

* * *

If you like **Psychological Thrillers,** join Detective Jamie Brooke and museum researcher Blake Daniel:

Desecration #1
Delirium #2
Deviance #3

* * *

For more **dark fantasy,** check out:

Risen Gods
The Dark Queen
A Thousand Fiendish Angels:
Short stories based on Dante's Inferno

More books coming soon.

You can sign up to be notified of new releases, giveaways and pre-release specials - plus, get a free book!

www.JFPenn.com/free

If you loved the book and have a moment to spare, I would really appreciate a short review on the page where you bought the book. Your help in spreading the word is gratefully appreciated and reviews make a huge difference to helping new readers find the series.

Thank you!

ABOUT J.F.PENN

J.F.Penn is the Award-nominated, New York Times and USA Today bestselling author of the ARKANE action adventure thrillers, Brooke & Daniel Psychological Thrillers, and the Mapwalker fantasy adventure series, as well as other stand-alone stories.

Her books weave together ancient artifacts, relics of power, international locations and adventure with an edge of the supernatural. Joanna lives in Bath, England and enjoys a nice G&T.

You can follow Joanna's travels on Instagram @jfpennauthor and also on her podcast at BooksAndTravel.page.

* * *

Sign up for your free thriller,
Day of the Vikings, and updates from behind
the scenes, research, and giveaways at:

www.jfpenn.com/free

* * *

Connect with Joanna:
www.JFPenn.com
joanna@JFPenn.com
www.Facebook.com/JFPennAuthor
www.Instagram.com/JFPennAuthor

* * *

For writers:

Joanna's site, www.TheCreativePenn.com, helps people write, publish and market their books through articles, audio, video and online courses.

She writes non-fiction for authors under Joanna Penn and has an award-nominated podcast for writers, The Creative Penn Podcast.

Printed in Great Britain
by Amazon

31552592R00121